Terrible Claw

Jacob Russell Dring

"These creatures' popularity grows each year… because a skeleton of a [dinosaur] still has the ability, even 65 million years after its death, to chill us to the bone."

Ray Harryhausen

"Fear is a place where you just tell the truth."

Clive Barker

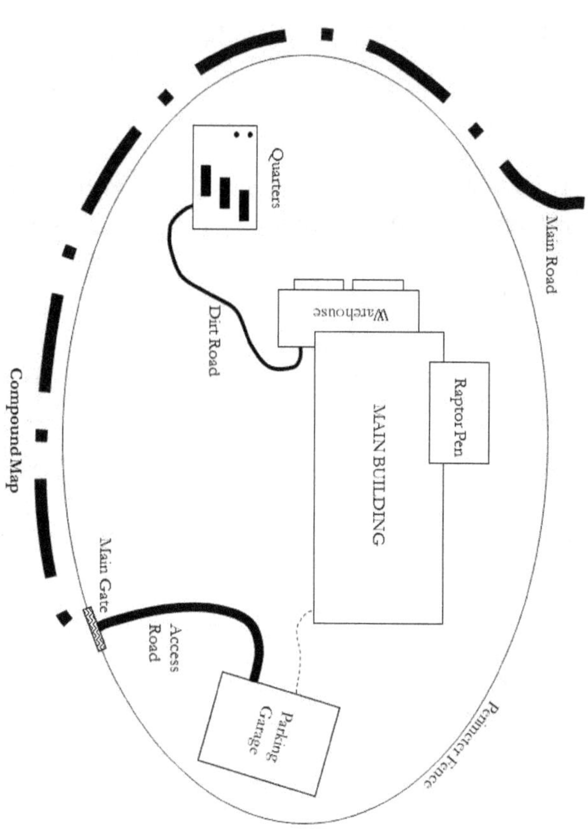

Main Road
Compound Map
Quarters
Dirt Road
Warehouse
Raptor Pen
MAIN BUILDING
Main Gate
Access Road
Parking Garage
Perimeter Fence

1

The creature's thick, muscular tongue curled up from its sublingual fold, carrying a moist, dense, shrill sound. It rose from its lungs, vibrating through the larynx, and echoed in the holding cell. This trilling was the creature's expression of discontent. A myriad emotion at its simplest. Unease, which could evolve into either fear or anger, or the sheer tumult of adrenaline.

Creatures like her were oblivious to most shades of fear, though. She knew so little about life beyond her pen, which was only about a tenth of an acre. All that she could extrapolate was from the half-ton cows fed to her and the others. And the upright species that provided the food.

Ironic, considering they were edible, too.

And more easily masticated, more easily digested. And, supposing she could process such an emotion, more *fun* to consume.

What certainly didn't help their situation of being on the menu was their continual mistreatment of her and the others. From prodding with or without added electricity, to teasing or entirely withholding food, and even periods of confinement. The latter was usually associated with light deprivation and sound torture.

The upright species were the cause of everything unjust that she and the others had experienced since they were juveniles. Through their infancy, they were coddled and treated humanely.

This was short-lived.

Maturing rapidly and fiercely, she and the others soon found themselves more capable than their infant selves could have ever fathomed.

Thus came the prodding.

The upright species never shied from mistreating her and the others.

Eventually, she really had no reason to resist. The first time one of them fell into the pen, the others had the pleasure of testing its anatomy. There was never a second time, although her observation of the others *had* kindled a curiosity in her.

And then one of her "handlers" left his arm in the fence for too long. A whole half second too long. Even in knowing the fence was electrified, she treated herself to a taste at the expense of a few thousand volts jolting through her neck.

The bereavement of her handler's arm awarded her a deep sleep thanks to a tranquilizer dart, and even more voltage via prodding for the next week.

She had, however, not forgotten the taste.

Besides, what was a week in the face of three years?

Hestia had matured faster than the others, although her male counterparts were not lesser beasts for it. At least, not that much less.

She wasn't aware of her name.

Her consciousness had no grasp of language, although her handlers shouting that same word, over the course of years, registered that it was their label for her. But nothing more.

The others had labels, too.

She deduced it was so that the upright species—the humans—could keep track of them. Could take notes and maintain records.

Hestia didn't care what the humans called her or the others. The only thing that mattered was their inferiority, their false sense of protection, and their…

Tenderness.

"How's our starlet doing this evening?" Dr. Lewis Campbell asked, strolling into the paddock above the pen. He adjusted his glasses, which fit his tall, rectangular head almost eccentrically, and smirked.

"She's still in her holding cell, Doctor," one of his med-techs replied, wielding a clipboard. "As per your instructions."

"Oh, but of course. Sixteen hours is almost up. She'll be most excited to stretch her legs in the pen."

Campbell was already wearing his lab coat, its spotless white fabric the only thing about him that was untarnished. The look in his graying blue eyes had for the longest time started to deteriorate in morality, although most of his colleagues remained loyal to him.

Most.

The too few that had their doubts were, at this point, shamefully complicit with his misdeeds.

"The second you sign that NDA," he had told them upon employment, "you're in this for the long run."

There were other insinuated threats, some vaguer than others, but it was all a given regardless. What the formerly award-winning geneticist had undertaken, and the applications he sought for his project, could only be interpreted as unethical. The latter, at least. His initial goal bred excitement and disbelief in his colleagues, which he used to reel them in.

Even after a slew of failures, from botched births to irreversible defects in juveniles which led to terminations, Dr. Campbell's tenacity prevailed.

The miracle that was recreating a dinosaur had finally been achieved, through his radical genius. It was merely a shame that he had chosen to pursue it privately, which was inherent to his plan from the beginning.

A plan that only he and his assistant were truly aware of.

Although months from accomplishing his own doctorate, Glen Isaacs gave up that dream in exchange for another. Helping his colleague and friend achieve the impossible. Resurrecting an animal from Cretaceous extinction, and not just one.

Hestia wasn't even the first.

Victor was, hence his name. The first of the males, and the first ever genetically engineered, reborn *Deinonychus antirrhopus*. A victory for the field of paleontology, zoology, and biotechnology. While, simultaneously, an affront to all three.

Because Victor, along with his other "subjects," were not encoded to be one-hundred-percent historically accurate. Of course, paleo-accuracy was an ever-changing dilemma within the community, but it was more than that.

Dr. Campbell sought different changes, of which he offered his curious lab-techs various reasons. Or, in his mind, excuses.

Whether out of fear or naïveté, they bought in and proceeded.

With Isaacs' help, Campbell never really had to repeat himself. Though shy of his doctorate, Isaacs was nonetheless acclaimed in the field of biotechnology.

He wasn't the only one recruited by Campbell to be a star player in his or her field. Campbell had managed to employ some of the best up-and-comers across the nation, within the medical community. From hematologists to toxicologists to pathologists.

Within months of renovating the abandoned hospital on Route 7 in Indiana, Campbell had allocated an impressive staff. In the weeks that would follow, he would accrue more, many of whom signed on before their services were even required.

Afterall, Campbell had to consider the future.

He would need a skeleton crew to ensure functionality of the hospital-turned-compound, who of course would have the least amount of knowledge regarding the project.

Eventually he had two janitors and two cargo drivers on his payroll. The latter would also load and unload various equipment, half of which might have seemed suspicious, but their NDA comfortably balanced with their paychecks.

The two IT personnel he ultimately hired came as recommendations of Isaacs. They were young but capable and ambitious. Most importantly, signed their contracts with enthusiasm.

Campbell's primary essential staff would be the most critical of his employees. Along with Isaacs, they would help him materialize his vision.

Two med-techs who were not too young but old enough to have some form of desperation in their veins. Most importantly, desperate to be a part of something momentous.

Elijah Hall and Ida Salanueva.

Over the years, their loyalty never seemed to wane in Campbell's eyes. Both of them revered his ambition, genius, and tenacity.

Virtually everyone at the compound did, on some level or another. Thanks to investments contributed by half of them, cost wasn't much of an issue once construction was completed. Campbell's savings were all but siphoned, and he could begin working.

It had not been long before major progress was underway. Witch each victory came fleeting waves of incredulity among his staff. However, their dedication subsisted. For they all knew, or believed in, the recognition and awards they would receive once Campbell publicized his project.

What might likely be criticized by some would be applauded by most.

This was what drove them.

Between Campbell and Isaacs, however, it was a little more than that. It was power.

"It's a big day, folks," Campbell announced, reminding them. Given, the day had almost come and gone. It was 4:40 in the afternoon, but Campbell had been running diagnostics and preparing for tonight, in his office, all day.

Hands clasped behind his back, he strode over to where Isaacs stood, by the paddock windows. They were tall and wide, three spacious panels overlooking the electric-fenced pen, like a basket of foliage and trees spanning five-thousand square feet below.

The pen itself was situated at the rear of the compound, geographically contained by a high ridgeline. Which was in addition to the perimeter fencing surrounding the property.

Campbell's eyes scanned the overlapping trees, the tallest of which didn't exceed the pen's twelve-foot fences.

Visibility from the paddock was still minimal, as the creatures favored using the foliage to their advantage. As if they knew they were being constantly studied.

Thus, the infrared readout on the control panel was often referred. While scientists spent the last few years dissolving fossils to inspect living tissue in hopes of determining whether dinosaurs were warm-blooded, cold-blooded, endothermic, or exothermic, Dr. Campbell and his staff knew the truth.

Or at least their version of it.

Deinonychus were, despite their reptilian traits, warm-blooded. More faithful to their avian DNA.

"How is Horace looking?" Campbell asked. "I know how antsy he gets when Hestia isn't in the pen."

"Quite, but not today. He seems a little more re-served." Isaacs' eyebrows raised. "Perhaps he…knows something, Doctor."

Campbell practically scoffed.

"Doubtful. The only ones that show heightened in-telligence are Hestia and Kilo. And Kilo, not anywhere near *her*."

"True," Isaacs said, beginning to add "but," how-ever, biting his tongue and suppressing it. If he was to contradict the Doctor, it would be done privately, not in front of Elijah and Ida.

"And the others?"

"I suspect Scar knows it's almost feeding time," Isaacs said, with a small smirk. He indicated a thermal readout on the screen that was marked as Scar-08. The eighth birth. "He's been keeping to himself with a sense of…patience."

Their names had meanings, Scar being the most overt. At only six months old, then known as DA-08, the male attempted to court Hestia. Horace, then known as DA-05, "defended" Hestia, clawing 08 over his left eye. He suffered partial blindness, although it had little effect on his target acquisition. Since then, 08 became Scar, and 05 became Horace, named after a famous Roman poet.

All of their names, save Victor and Kilo, were as-signed by Campbell himself. Victor's came about as a collective across the staff, amid their celebration of the first healthy birth. Kilo's was merely the result of a joke by Isaacs, since he was the heaviest at birth. And, to this day, the largest of the males, though still a few feet shy of Hestia's length.

Named after the Greek goddess of sacrificial fire and chastity, Hestia was the only female *Deinonychus* engineered, albeit following two terminal defects. Her growth, both physically and mentally, instilled awe in everyone involved.

Campbell looked at her with pure marvel.

Hestia was also unique in her sex. Though female by design, she was coded to be infertile. This would be detected by the males to abolish infighting and any attempts at mating, while still heeding her as their superior.

Her size and intelligence solidified this plan.

The males, on the other hand, were engineered with protandrous hermaphrodism, allowing them to switch to female in a single-sex environment, in order to procreate. So long as Hestia was around—not just in the vicinity, but alive, and it had been established that they could tell—the males would remain.

Although called by some as a dangerous "fighting fire with fire" maneuver in the lab, Isaacs was supportive of Campbell's decision. He called it "an ambitious risk of genius."

The others fell in line.

"Kilo, Victor, and Six are themselves. Lazy, but not idle."

"Good. I suppose it's time to remind them they're alive, then." Campbell nodded at Isaacs, and then withdrew.

He turned to face Elijah and Ida.

"Salanueva, would you do the honor?"

"Absolutely, Doctor," she said, and reached for the landline. She picked up the receiver and dialed seven. The intercom beeped. "Dinnertime, main pen. Dinnertime, main pen. Thank you."

She hung up the phone and exchanged courteous smiles with Campbell.

As opposed to announcing that it was "feeding time for the *raptors*," they chose a vaguer route. This way, any non-essential personnel would only have their wild deductions and imaginations to fill in the gaps. It was already assumed that Dr. Campbell's compound was for some level of animal testing.

Those not directly involved with the genetic engineering and maintenance of the live creatures were not in the know. Nor could they possibly come close to fathoming resurrected dinosaurs.

Besides, "raptor" was an informal term seldom used by Campbell and his staff. The *Deinonychus* was a genus of dromaeosaur, among which included the much smaller *Velociraptor* and the even larger *Utahraptor*, which Hestia and Kilo more accurately represented. When not using their given names, the creatures were typically referred to as "subjects."

Ida's intercom announcement brought into motion the feeding of the raptors. If done as a group, as it would be this evening, Hestia would first be relocated to the main pen.

Campbell's plan for tonight was only explicitly known by Isaacs. Elijah and Ida simply knew that there would be "the first test of its kind" in a few hours, and eagerly awaited more details.

Between Campbell and Isaacs, the circumstances of tonight's test required unity among the creatures. Therefore returning Hestia to the group was essential, and it was the Doctor's belief that confining her for the past sixteen hours would intensify their bond.

A perfect catalyst for tonight's test.

The second they heard Ida's announcement, Hestia's three handlers got to work. While experienced in working with crocodiles and Komodo dragons, the three men had to undergo intense training and overcome their own fears to competently manage such a creature. First they conquered their shock and awe of witnessing a live dinosaur in the flesh, and then they focused on their paychecks.

Of all the employees under Campbell's wing, these three were the most fueled by sheer adrenaline. They did, however, have a different perspective of the raptors than the plethora of lab-techs working for the Doctor. They saw the creatures as both magnificent and petrifying. Worthy of the name *Deinonychus*.

Ancient Greek for "terrible claw."

Their eponymous scythe-like toe-claws were, still, not the worst of their nature. The pointed jaws lined with slightly curved, horribly sharp teeth and their darting yellow eyes were possibly the most distressing to witness in the flesh.

And then came feeding time.

Seeing how the creatures behaved when food was readily available would proceed to give the handlers nightmares for months. Suffice it to say, their hands would impulsively grip their electric batons tighter.

The three handlers did not just "take care of" Hestia, but the others as well. As part of their NDA, before employment, the men had to agree on two major additions to the usual privacy conditions.

One, to treat the animals as per the Doctor's direction, without question or objection, period. This would later entail the arguable mistreatment of the animals, which Campbell claimed was to "enhance aggression," and thus benefit the creatures' application. These acts, however, were kept from the knowledge of Elijah and Ida, fearing their moral qualms.

And two, to perform their duties in lieu of obvious health risks. This included the statement of a previous handler's death, before the third was hired, as a replacement.

Seamus O'Connor and Alec Carter had witnessed their coworker's death, when he fell into the pen during crane maintenance. The crane was used to lower live cattle into the pen during feeding time. There was a malfunction, and one of the handlers insisted on fixing the crane, as he had in the past. Only this time, Kilo leapt onto the lowered gurney, from which the cow had previously been torn from in a frenzy, thus shaking the handler from the crane.

His demise was witnessed by O'Connor and Carter from outside the pen, below the paddock, as well as Campbell and Isaacs.

Elijah and Ida were not direct witnesses, though they would claim that the cacophony sufficed.

The poor soul's replacement as the third *Deinonychus* handler was Juan Martín, who shared a similar verve and vigor that the other two began with. Since, they would be lying if they said these same emotions had not dwindled.

Relocating Hestia was quite a chore.

Once it was a challenge and burden among everything else, but over the last few months it had simply become routine. Albeit an extremely taxing one.

Hestia was herded into a reinforced cage aligned on a monorail system that transported the subject—be it her or any of the males, though always one at a time—to the pen. Medical diagnoses and other treatments were always conducted in the confined holding cells, most of which required heavy sedation.

Hestia and Kilo required more, while the others, even Scar, who was inarguably the most reckless of the subjects, would go under with the normal dosage.

The path of the monorail cage kept it from both visibility and earshot of nonessential personnel.

Altogether, the compound's daily staff during working hours consisted of nineteen, including Campbell himself, but excluding the two drivers and two janitors.

Among the Doctor's essential personnel, albeit outside of the medical field, were the compound's primary security. Cillian Gage had the highest ranking before his discharge as a Ranger seven years ago. This was enough for Osvaldo Ramirez and Tate Anderssen to see him as their leader. Although it was Gage and Anderssen who established their private military contractor group, more close-knitted than most PMCs, Ramirez was hired months later.

The three men had a similar awe for the raptors as their handlers, but at far less risk.

Anytime a raptor was transported within the compound, two of the security team were attached as a safeguard. The third was posted outside of the pen, an uneventful position they called a sentry.

While rotating shifts were advised, Anderssen insisted on being the sentry, after only one experience escorting a caged raptor. It had been Scar, whose appearance alone was even more unsettling than the larger Hestia or Kilo. Not to mention its aggression; Scar was unquestionably the most energetic of the six, at all times. Often taunting the handlers and "going ape-shit," as O'Connor once said, during feeding time.

More than the others, that was.

Nothing eventful had happened that day, but witnessing Scar's aggression even by itself sufficed to shake Anderssen to his core.

The other two contractors didn't argue. They were unnerved on their own level, but after a few months treated the beasts as nothing more than "mutant reptiles."

Of course, dromaeosaurs were more avian in nature and physiology than reptiles, but Dr. Campbell had bypassed this in the genetics phase. He instructed his staff to prioritize the reptilian DNA used to fill in the gaps in code. Most female reptiles were larger than the males, and less colorful. These same traits carried over to the *Deinonychus*, leaving Hestia to be a few feet longer, snout to tail, and taller at the shoulder, while sporting a duller, unmarked brown complexion.

Campbell's intention.

His choice to design the creatures devoid of feathers was, as he debated his hired paleontologist, grounded by reason. Foremost, feathers in recreation could be an unnecessary obstacle, with complications in keratin density and ingrown or congested follicles.

This was merely Campbell's preliminary excuse. His primary was rooted in practicality and control.

Without feathers, the *Deinonychus* could not attack as scientists and animal behaviorists theorized. Latching onto their prey and using their winged arms to hover, while eating it alive. Although terrifying to imagine, the potential risk of a subject achieving any level of flight complicated containment issues.

Campbell's only other reason was actually his primary, but knowledge of it was only shared by Isaacs.

The absence of feathers would let the dinosaur DNA favor its base skin impressions—a pebbled, leathery reptilian hide. The males, although more colorful than Hestia, were not remotely as flamboyant as their plumage could have been. This would be disastrous in Campbell's eyes, as he sought to design sleek, covert predators.

"Besides," he added, in a secret conversation with Isaacs, "they're scarier this way."

It was blunt and he half-expected Isaacs to react unsavorily. Much to his surprise, and delight, Campbell witnessed only accordance in his colleague.

Anderssen's insistence on being the sentry whenever a raptor was transferred from holding cell to pen, and vice versa, was further proof. Campbell never questioned Anderssen's commitment to his NDA, especially since he was Gage's right-hand, but knowing that the man had nightmares of what the Doctor actually *dreamt* of, pleased him.

That staff like Elijah and Ida couldn't detect this level of sadism was their own fault. They were blinded by the wonderment of what they had helped produce; while not wholly true to dinosaurian history, the subjects were accurate enough.

They saw this project as nothing shy of miraculous. Yet, in the chasms of their minds, buried sentiments whispered.

This project was an affront to nature.

Day in and night out, this inner voice was suppressed by their awe of what they helped create. It was primarily the Doctor's genius, but without their assistance, investments, and tenacity through trial and error, he would never have succeeded.

This was as humbling as it was nerve-wracking, whenever feeding time came around. Always conducted in the later hours of the afternoon, calling it "dinner" was appropriate.

They were not necessarily nocturnal by nature, but Campbell had helped structure them this way. Through a series of sleep deprivation tests, and then feeding them just before it got dark, thus heightening their blood pressure and heartrates, he conditioned the raptors to be nocturnal. Their eyesight was superior than a human's in low lighting, without any additional changes to their DNA. As far as Campbell was concerned, he was simply "reminding" the creatures of their "purpose."

Hestia was, to most of the staff's surprise, fairly calm during her caged return to the pen.

When the cage sealed to the pen's umbilical gate, which then lifted with a magnetic hiss, she reentered the pen with zeal.

"See Horace? How his head lifts, but he doesn't move from his corner?" Campbell drummed a capped pen on his lips. His rectangular glasses sat low on the bridge of his nose. "Yes. He knows she's back, but doesn't want to seem…desperate."

"And then there's Scar," Isaac smirked. He tracked the heat signature of Scar-08, as it darted around the pen. Weaving between trees and through fern clusters. "Not sure if he's excited or just being Scar."

"Maybe even agitated," Campbell said, shrugging and turning his back on the paddock windows. Ida was facing the wall, doing paperwork, and didn't notice Dr. Campbell sizing her up. She had a lean frame and the white lab coat offered nothing, especially from the back. Yet still Campbell ogled.

Elijah, meanwhile, was in the far corner, at a computer terminal, enrapt in his work. Even as Campbell and Isaacs exchanged words.

The Doctor's eyes were locked onto Ida, particularly her exposed ears and nape, just above the white coat collar, her dark brown hair in a pixie cut.

"How do you mean?" Isaacs finally asked, not removing his attention from the infrared readout.

"Perhaps," Campbell said, his focus unwavering as well, "Scar is envious. Of Hestia's power. Not just in general, but over the others. And her…dominion…when it comes to the feast."

"Ah," it clicked in Isaacs. He leaned forward, peering through the glass and glimpsing movement among the shuddering foliage. The raptors began to convene in their own scattered manner, chirping, growling, and trilling at each other. "You think he's disappointed she's back, just in time for their meal? That he'll now get less. Because of her."

Elijah's hands relented on his keyboard, seconds before looking up from the computer. At the same time, Ida began to turn.

Campbell cleared his throat and faced the paddock windows again.

"Quite possibly," he said.

"Interesting observation, Doctor," Isaacs said.

"Where is that damn meat?" Campbell sighed.

"Should I page again, Doctor?" Ida asked.

Without turning, Campbell shook his head and waved a hand over his shoulder.

"No, no. It'll be here. I suppose waiting even longer ought to work out better, anyway."

Both Ida and Elijah's faces were torn with ambivalence. They respected the ingenuity behind Dr. Campbell's radical experiments, to test the animals and observe their behavioral variances. But they also felt for the raptors, beyond being just subjects in a controlled environment.

No matter how fierce and debatably merciless they had become.

"Ah, here it is," Isaacs said, nodding.

A crane, manually operated from a secure glass and steel cabin just outside the pen, pivoted the raptors' evening meal above the fences. Usually it was a nine-hundred-pound cow, fresh off sedation, so that it wouldn't panic. And so that the raptors wouldn't digest any of the drug, residually. By the time the cow was lowered into the pen completely, the raptors would be all over it, often leaping at it even before.

Still, the crane operator would wait until its hooves were on the ground, presumably anyway, before detaching the gurney. This way they could prohibit damage to the crane, and retrieve the shredded canvas gurney later.

Except this afternoon was different.

Menu wise.

Neither Ida nor Elijah were too pleased about the confinement of Hestia for sixteen hours, but it was acceptable. The reduction of their meal, however, seemed more like torture than experiment.

Six adult raptors needed adequate nourishment. Their aggression had been recorded as peaking, in the past, when they received less.

The sheep bleated in the gurney as it was lowered into the pen. Already the raptors beneath warbled and hissed with disappointment. They could tell. This wasn't right. It had to be a mistake, right? No. No, this was merely an appetizer. A reward for their behavior, especially Hestia's, despite her confinement.

No more than three-hundred pounds, the shorn sheep bleated less once it was let down all the way. The crane operator disengaged the gurney and lifted the mechanical arm up, clearing the pen.

Seconds passed, and the raptors had not launched themselves at the animal.

This troubled Isaacs slightly, but piqued Campbell's intrigue.

He pondered if they thought this was some kind of trick, or if they did in fact wonder that it was another test. At any rate, Scar was too impatient to play by Hestia's rules, supposing she was the one who communicated that they wait.

He released a vaulting snarl that sounded like nails on a chalkboard, as he leapt from cover and pounced the sheep.

The others followed suit, eager to get their fair share of meat from the helpless animal.

Heavy breathing and the tearing of flesh ensued. Raptor bodies slammed into each other, and vegetation tore from their roots amid the frenzy.

The sheep's heat signature faded from the infrared readout. Thermal stripes adorning leaves and soil. Blood everywhere, and on the raptors themselves. Which would soon be licked clean, by each other or themselves.

"Beautiful," Campbell muttered, within earshot of only Isaacs.

"Doctor?" Isaacs said, leaning in to exchange a few private words. "You think that will be enough to tide them over?"

"Hardly," Campbell smiled, pushing his glasses up his nose. "But that's the point, now, isn't it?"

Gage, Ramirez, and Anderssen returned from the secondary quarters outside of the main compound. There, Campbell's hired third-party security team, call-sign Bravo, were housed. Three trailer buildings, two beds and one shower within each, were arranged with very little space between them. The two outhouses within the high, square perimeter walls didn't make it any easier. Bravo claimed that it felt like an internment camp.

Far worse than the employment situation of Campbell's on-site security team. Gage, Ramirez, and Anderssen were able to pack it up every night and return home.

The exact reason for hiring additional security, and not being tasked as overnight sentries, eluded the three men. And even the six PMCs of Bravo.

Their paychecks were comforting, though.

Sure…Dr. Campbell gave off a weird energy, his NDA rousing suspicions, and the details of his work no less vague, but at least he was courteous.

Or so the men convinced themselves.

The advanced payment had definitely been reassuring. Only a few of the men had close family, although the details of their work kept separate from them. Those who had wives, children, or parents transferred their advances to them.

The final payment from Campbell, at the end of the week, would be twice their advance. This was only their second day, and the end of their first official "shift," spent patrolling the front perimeter. Yesterday, although paid for, had been the Doctor's guided tour of the compound.

A limited look at the exterior grounds of the structure, and of course their quarters. A walled-off square of land where they would retire every night.

According to Campbell, the twenty-foot perimeter wall was for blocking reception and thus ensuring part of the privacy policy in their NDA.

"Not that I don't trust you," he had said, with a weaselly smirk.

They constantly reminded themselves of the payment they had already received, and would at the end of the week. This, they looked forward to.

So far, it was a walk in the park.

Another part of their NDA, however, was most disquieting. They accepted it, ultimately, choosing to believe in Campbell's insistence that it was yet another "sealant of trust." No matter how much of a stretch that seemed.

"Are they just naïve, or got dollar signs in their eyes?" Ramirez asked, as the three men parked the Jeep behind the loading docks of the compound.

The quarters were fifty yards from the main building. Connected by a narrow dirt path. And only about twenty yards from the sole road that led to and from here, cutting through the Indiana country. Albeit on the other side of a perimeter fence circling the property.

Night had just fallen. There was still a hue of light

left in the scarce clouds suspended over the region.

"Maybe a bit of both," Anderssen said. He shut his door and helped Ramirez with the weapon cases.

Gage took one in each hand himself. He kicked his door shut, and then the passenger one behind him.

"Not both," Gage added, leading them up a ramp that entered the building just beside the warehouse. He held it open with his body as the others walked past.

"Why not?" Ramirez asked.

The cool air-conditioning in the hall, despite the dim lighting in this section of the compound at night, was nice on their faces. Gage had long hair, tied into a ponytail during his shift, under a backwards cap, and a light beard. Ramirez had a narrow goatee and short black hair. The blonde Anderssen was clean-shaven, feeling the A/C the most, although Gage was more grateful for it.

"These guys, we know so little about 'em, but they're contractors, too," Gage explained as he followed the others toward the armory. "Twice as big. We're talkin' six men, some with families, and dedicated. PMC work that pays this much for so little is cut and dry. Less questions, more money. That's how it works. They know this."

Anderssen, with one hand free, tapped in a code on the keypad beside the door, and it beeped. Then he put his shoulder into it, and pushed the heavy steel door open. He held it with a boot and the other two entered.

"It's not about naïveté," Gage continued, setting the weapons cases down on a counter. "Ignorance is bliss. Now be honest. After everything we've seen, don't you wish we had that liberty?"

No truer words had ever been spoken.

The men relished at that thought, and then proceeded with their task. They secured Bravo's weapons in their own cabinet, and then left the armory locked again in their wake.

They headed upstairs, making a routine walk to find the Doctor. His office was on the third floor, the compound's highest level below the roof. The opposite end of the building, on the same level, was his main lab, a paddock overlooking the raptor pen.

Expecting to knock on the always-locked door to his office, they instead bumped into him in the hallway en route. He was fast on his feet, clearly engaged in whatever tonight's big test was.

The three men were clueless, and okay with that. As Gage had insinuated back in the armory, having the privilege of complete knowledge was overrated.

Unlike most nights, however, their shift this evening didn't end when the sun went down. Instead, they were kept on for an additional two hours; this came with a small bonus, which no three could refuse.

Especially since, unlike Bravo, they were permitted to carry their weapons at all times during their shift. It was a minimal loadout for each man. Pistols on the hip and a few shotguns in the armory. Campbell's terms of employment restricted automatic weapons or rifles from crossing the main gate. He gave no reasons, which didn't bother the three men until they witnessed the growth of his "subjects."

Since then, they had at least been allowed to carry

shotguns during the relocation of any raptor via the monorail.

Bravo's accordance to this policy was slightly comforting, as it suggested that their presence was purely for peace-of-mind than actual firepower. Still, this didn't keep them from bringing a full arsenal of versatile handguns and shotguns.

"There you are!" Campbell seemed delighted to see his primary security team. More than usual. "I didn't get a chance to talk to Bravo after their first shift. How are they adjusting?"

"Like just another job, it seems," Gage said, nonchalantly.

"More uneventful than they expected, I imagine," Campbell nodded, squinting.

A pair of scientists carrying clipboards walked by, courteously nodding at the Doctor before veering into an office a few doors down.

Gage shrugged. "We're not all adrenaline junkies, Doctor. Most soldiers know every day can't be action-packed."

"Right, of course," Campbell nodded, not taking any offense from Gage's response, nor reading that he was offended, either. Campbell cleared his throat and clapped his hands together. "And your retrieval of their weapons, that's finished?"

Gage nodded. Ramirez coughed into his hands.

"Locked in the armory as you instructed," Gage said.

"How did they feel about?" Dr. Campbell, always analyzing.

"Not too happy. Can't say I don't blame 'em."

"Try not to pity them too much, Gage," Campbell said, making his way around the three men. "Or any of you, for that matter. Securing their weapons is solely a precaution."

"Understood," Gage shrugged. "It's your building, your work, Doc. But since we're staying a little longer tonight, might I ask what we're in store for?"

"Curiosity and the cat didn't pair so well, don't you know?" Campbell failed to suppress a wry smirk.

He didn't wait for the men to react, beyond glancing at each other, before giving a more direct answer.

"How about this? Take a load off in the breakroom. Ten, fifteen minutes. Then pick up and secure the posterior. Especially the docks, and warehouse. From the inside, though. Supposed to be a tad chilly tonight."

Campbell's last sentence was tinged with a sense of humor that slightly perturbed Gage. He wondered if the others caught onto it, but wouldn't pry.

Ignorance was bliss, afterall, wasn't it?

"You got it, Doc. And once we're done?"

"Just take your time. As soon as you're needed, I'll page for you. Thanks for your understanding."

"Of course," Gage nodded, and the others did, too. Then Campbell returned the gesture, smiling politely, and continued on his way.

Once the Doctor was past the corner and down the other hall, Anderssen stepped closer to have a quiet word. There was still an occasional med-tech walking past them every few seconds. At nightfall the compound was at its busiest, concluding the day's work.

"Well, that was fucking weird," Anderssen said.

"What going on around here *isn't*?" Gage said. Stating the obvious. Even still, it hit different tonight.

<u>3</u>

Ambivalence plagued Bravo. They settled into their beds—more like cots, one of them griped—and prepared to sleep. They would dream of money, and hate themselves for it. Never soldiers of fortune, fighting for no other purpose than to be paid, the six men had not known a job like this before. To be paid so handsomely and seemingly be of no use was difficult to grasp.

For most of them.

Eric Armijo was supposed to be their leader, the co-founder of the PMC group, with his childhood friend and brother-in-arms Cameron Fletcher. It was relieving that Fletcher had a similar attitude that he did; shrug it off, accept the paycheck, and be grateful for the low stress.

Beneath the surface, though, Armijo combatted the same emotions that the rest of his men voiced. The feeling of inadequacy, of uselessness, despite existing to serve a purpose, and serve it fervently.

Being relieved of their weapons overnight had been tentatively agreed upon. Armijo was comforted that he didn't need to convince the others himself, and that most of them eventually caved to the condition.

Some even articulated that it actually made sense—a stretch—from a precautionary perspective.

Armijo peered out of the window beside his bed, a sliding glass panel with ratty blinds over it. He bent one and scanned the dimness outside. His view was beautiful—he told himself, sarcastically. He saw the two outhouses, and from one emerged a man.

Channing Harbison yawned and made eye contact with his team leader. It would have been awkward for most, but for them it was nothing. Harbison waved lackadaisically as he moseyed back to his trailer, the farthest from Armijo's. Harbison "bunked" with Jordan Labella. The trailer between them was occupied by Josh Guidry and David Hsu.

Armijo withdrew from the window and settled into bed. At the opposite end of the trailer rested Fletcher, on his back with hands clasped under his head. He didn't seem too intent on falling asleep, oddly enough.

A few seconds after his head hit the pillow, it dawned on Armijo what "that sound" was. He had heard it earlier but not registered it.

One of the men was in the shower for some reason, despite their incredibly uneventful day. They still wore full gear during, no matter how minimal their arsenal was. Nonetheless…

He could hear the crank shower going, utilizing a water supply tank the size of a minivan outside the trailer. Judging by the faintness of the sound, he supposed it was Labella in the farthest.

"Do you know who the hell's in the shower?" Armijo asked, raising his voice a touch to be heard by Fletcher thirty feet away.

The lights were off in their trailer, but the compound's were still on, a subtle glow through the blinds over their two windows. It seemed most of its personnel were still busy wrapping up for the day. Armijo could even hear the distant hum of trucks or cranes putting in work. The main gate, and the access road that ran from it to the parking garage, were all on the opposite side of the property from Bravo's quarters.

So it wasn't like any of that *kept* them awake.

Besides, the solace of sleep had yet enticed Fletcher.

Most of the men in Bravo were light sleepers, unfortunately.

Hsu was notorious for being able to achieve REM in record time, no matter the amount of noise or lights.

"Probably Labella," Fletcher chuckled. "You know how that man sweats up a storm."

Armijo smirked and shook his head.

"Goddamn," he muttered, and tried to get comfortable.

Dr. Campbell knew it wasn't the wisest decision to indulge his entire staff about tonight's plan. But as the raptors were being caged and transported, one by one, into the shipping container outside of the pen, he acknowledged the necessity of full disclosure.

Most of the non-essential personnel were on their way out of the building, and home, at this point. Ten minutes ago he had made the announcement via the intercom, wishing everyone a good night and thanking them for their continued dedication.

It was a polite way of saying "get the fuck out."

Their drive home would be at least twenty minutes, as it was no less than that to the nearest sign of civilization. There was no wonder why the original building, once a hospital, had been lost to debt and eventually ruin.

Although the records weren't as public as he would have liked, Campbell couldn't help but wonder if the place was used for mental patients. Or potentially dangerous ones.

Part of him hoped this was the case.

He enjoyed a little bit of irony.

Meanwhile, his own "patients" were impatiently herded into a lightless shipping container. The interior had been densely padded, so as to reduce the animals' own damage in transit, and to eliminate excessive noise. He of course knew it would only be a matter of minutes before the floor padding was torn up by their claws.

"I-I don't believe this," Ida's response to the news. She looked at her colleague. Elijah was having trouble processing it as well, but not nearly as disquietly as her. She eventually shoved him. "Are you as aloof as they are!?"

Elijah took a deep breath, and raised a palm to her, implying she calm down. He didn't want to get physical. Elijah wasn't a large man. He was tall, but lean, with an average build that suggested lassitude in most of his life.

There was still something hidden about his demeanor, which raised the question of what exactly Elijah was capable of if pushed too far.

"I just think…" He started, his cheeks slowly getting rosier. "We should hear him out. Afterall, *Ida*, we *did* sign a non-disclosure—"

She shoved him again, and he almost fell into the computer terminal. A stack of papers scattered across the white tile floor of the paddock.

She marched toward the door.

Campbell sighed, not flinching.

It was Isaacs who stepped in her path, his tall frame and far reach alone blocking the doorway.

"You're being…unreasonable, Salanueva."

"Says the man who is all too calm in allowing such an enormity."

"I am not *pleased* about it. I am not *celebrating* the event. I'm merely…observing the scientific prospects."

"Scientific?" She scoffed, chuckling nervously before looking at Campbell. His hands in his lab coat pockets, a distant smugness on his face. She looked back at Isaacs. "If you call this *scientific*, I can't imagine what you consider *horrific*. Or if anything registers at all."

She scowled and shook her head, trying to worm her way past Isaacs.

And then one of Campbell's toxicologists appeared on the other side of the doorway. Isaacs withdrew, and straightened his lab coat. He nodded at the woman, who wore her own. She had dirty blonde hair, cropped high off her shoulders.

Janice Murphy cleared her throat.

She waved her clipboard before addressing Campbell, who lifted his chin, smiling a little.

"Doctor, just wanted to let you know—"

"Janice, oh God," Ida blurted, jostling past Isaacs to take a fistful of Janice's coat. "You're gonna think I'm crazy, but please listen to me, they're going to…they're…"

And then it hit Ida. She saw it on Janice's unfazed face. The mother of three already knew. Janice was not necessarily one of Campbell's essential staff, but if she knew then Ida suspected that most of the others did, too. Those that had not already been dismissed.

Ida let go of Janice and looked at Campbell.

"Who all…?"

"Hold that thought, Salanueva," the Doctor insisted. "Murphy? You were saying?"

"Right, I just wanted to inform you that I was finished for the day."

"Wonderful," Campbell said, hands softly coming together in front of him. "And the tranquilizers?"

"The darts have all been prepared, and I went over everything with the handlers."

"Excellent. Thank you so much, Murphy. See you tomorrow."

They exchanged handshakes, and Ida glimpsed a smile on Janice's face. It made her nauseous.

"Good luck, Doctor," she said, and then gave Isaacs a courteous nod before leaving.

Ida worked it over in her head faster than any calculation she had ever processed.

Before Janice got farther than ten feet from the door, Ida called her name. She paused, her pumps squeaking against the mottled brown tile.

"I…can you accompany me to the restroom?" Ida asked. She then touched her temple. "I think I need a moment."

Campbell tried not to smirk too hard. He waved off Isaacs' suspicious expression, and then gestured Ida go ahead. He walked into the doorway, behind her.

"If you don't mind, before you leave, Murphy. Thank you."

"Of course," Janice smiled, brow furrowed, as if it was absolutely no issue.

Ida tried to play it as cool as she could muster, which included burying her own humanity.

Just for a moment.

They reached the ladies' restroom on the third floor, two hallways from the paddock lab, and Ida washed her face.

"I know, it's a lot to take in, but you have to try and weigh the variables here," Janice said, behind her. "You might not have kids, but someday you'll want to, and you'll have the money to give them the best possible life. And if that's not enough, you'll be able to pride yourself with the achievements that Dr. Campbell has made possible. Remember, Ida…you were *chosen*. We all were. We owe him our devotion, and if not him, then the animals."

Ida looked at herself in the mirror, water dripping off her face.

She nodded and then dried off with a paper towel, before facing Janice.

"You're right, Janice, I'm so sorry I…" She chuckled nervously. "I freaked out, I just. Whew."

"Aw, don't worry, dear. This time tomorrow we'll be busy with so much new data and a whole fresh page of progress."

Janice put her hands on Ida's arms, and then turned to leave.

"I'll see you in the morning," she bid farewell.

"Have a good night," Ida said, and the second she heard the door shut, she entered the far stall and locked the door. She dug her phone out of a pocket, popped out the SIM card, useless within the walls of the compound.

Her ex-boyfriend used to work for the Corps, now he was with ASPCA. Before a month ago, she hadn't spoken to him in four years. But after growing suspicious of Campbell, she made contact.

Even then she felt like she was being watched.

Ida sat on the toilet, facing the back, using the lid as a workspace.

She reached under her shirt, and removed a SIM card from the wiring in her bra. She put it into the phone and dialed her ex.

The ringtone was choppy, and cut out after three seconds.

She cursed under her breath, her chest heaving.

Ida's mind worked fast.

Her head turned, and she found herself staring at the wall. But she wasn't looking at the wall. She was pushing her sight beyond it.

Armijo thought he had sunken into the cool embrace of sleep when the landline in the trailer rang. It was louder than any phone ought to be, jarring him wide awake and making Fletcher look at the wall mount with disdain. But also puzzlement.

The white glow of the compound's exterior lights, emanating just over the quarters' perimeter wall, remained. Armijo glanced at the window on his way to the ringing phone. Through the blinds, the distant glow told him that the compound was still occupied.

"You think we might actually be of service?" Fletcher asked from his bed, sitting up.

They practically had to yell to be heard over the ringing.

"Can't say I'd be relieved. Actually wanted to get some shut-eye." Armijo flipped one of the two ceiling fixtures on in the trailer. There was a table between the two beds, in the center of the structure, beside a small refrigerator.

"Don't lie to yourself," Fletcher smirked.

Armijo shook his head and lazily picked up the phone from the wall-mounted cradle.

"Yeah, this is Bravo. What's—"

A woman's hushed yet assertive voice pushed through the receiver. Immediately Armijo's rigid brow furrowed and he looked at Fletcher with bemusement legible on his face.

"Listen to me! In ten minutes, maybe less, you'll be in grave danger. First—"

"*Who* is this?" Armijo said, practically scoffing. He wasn't buying it. Someone in the compound pulling his chain.

Maybe a test of Dr. Campbell's, to rattle Bravo's cage and see just how grounded their loyalty was.

"Nevermind who, just *trust* me," she insisted.

The call wasn't the clearest, and static conquered the background. But her voice was adamant, and her inflection suggested that she was either serious, or a great actress.

"Are you armed?" She asked.

Armijo glanced at Fletcher. He had swung his legs off the side of the bed but sat there, quizzical.

Despite his previous inclination, Armijo was going to call her bluff. He scoffed and turned toward the wall mount.

"Nice try, lady. I'm hanging up."

"Fine!" She snapped. She proceeded to talk fast but with aggressive lucidity. "I work for Dr. Campbell. In about ten minutes he's going to cut the power to your quarters. Then he's going to unleash them."

Armijo's brow furrowed again.

His heart began to race, although he wasn't too sure why. Except that his questionable trust in the Good Doctor suddenly seemed to have merit.

"Unleash who?" When he asked it, he couldn't help but chuckle. He shook his head. "Look, this is nuts. I can't believe I'm talking to some prank ca—"

"The raptors!" The woman practically shouted. "The *Deinonychus*! Are you armed or not?"

"Uh…our weapons aren't on-site. It's part of Campbell's contract when we aren't on duty."

"Oh, no." Her voice sank. "Oh my God…"

Armijo cleared his throat and turned toward Fletcher. He was standing up, now, in his black Under-Armour briefs and compression shirt.

They made eye contact as Armijo spoke, and certain words widened Fletcher's eyes.

"You said *raptors*. Like…dinosaurs?" Armijo chuckled, nervously. "Do you really expect me to believe that shit?"

"I don't care what you believe in, you and your men are in *danger*! He doesn't know I'm calling you, but in less than ten minutes you're—"

The light turned off, and the woman's voice ended mid-breath. Replaced by silence.

Armijo removed the receiver from his ear and stared at it. Then he looked around the dark trailer. Fletcher stood by the fridge, holding the door open. The light was off and its normal hum was dead.

"The hell?" He said out loud.

Armijo glanced at the window. The glow of lights from the compound was still present. He wasn't sure if this was comforting or unsettling.

Everything that the woman had said began to sink in on a whole other level. A tingling sensation trickled down his spine.

"Fletcher," he said. "Put some clothes on."

4

Not just clothes. It wasn't technically against Campbell's NDA to carry knives on them, as their contract simply stated "no firearms when off-duty." Once Fletcher had secured his pants in haste, Armijo opposite him and following suit, he strapped a five-inch tactical knife, sheathed in its scabbard, to his thigh. It was not kept in some ceiling panel or beneath his mattress, only under his pillow.

Armijo's was as well.

Unfortunately, not all of them carried.

Most of the men had argued, after agreeing to this particular job, that it simply wasn't necessary. Their optimism was a virtue, not a weakness, which Armijo often wished he had.

Not tonight.

He didn't know what exactly was going on, but that woman's frantic voice had not finished doing a number on his nerves.

"We need to get a hold of the others," Armijo said. "Quietly, if possible."

"Throw me your flashlight," Fletcher said, walking to the window. He was fully dressed. He had even pulled a lightweight ballistic vest over his shirt.

Armijo had not gotten that far, and wasn't sure he

wanted to jump to such a paranoid conclusion. He was lacing up his boots when Fletcher made the request. He paused to dig his hands into a small bag beside a bedframe leg.

"Christ Almighty, what the hell is that?" Fletcher asked, two fingers bending the blinds to peer through the window. Armijo noticed his eyes were up, but not directly.

Fletcher looked toward the right corner of the window. A large shipping container secured by some kind of magnetic forklift was raised above the perimeter wall. The doors had been replaced with some kind of gate, which was raised.

"What?" Armijo asked, standing. "What is it?"

The container was the size of one of their trailers, sufficiently blocking the lights from the compound. Thus the contents, if any, weren't clear. The two men gawked up at it, their eyes searching for some kind of answer to their questions within the darkness.

Movement.

And then a loud, shrill sound that vibrated in the air. Guttural despite its high pitch.

Armijo and Fletcher flinched, startled by the sound alone, impulsively looking away as their faces contorted.

Shapes descended from the container, shapes they did not see. Blurs of motion from the corners of their eyes. Something heavy struck the roof of their trailer, startling them tenfold. They reflexively ducked, Fletcher on the ground, anticipating an explosion or something worse.

The warbling sounds continued, in bursts, but not as loud as before, somehow. And scattered. Above them, and somewhere off to the side.

They heard a loud crash, half-expecting it to be their own trailer, but were quick to realize it wasn't.

The men exchanged dumbstruck glances.

"Bravo," Armijo muttered.

He hated even calling themselves that. It was a call-sign given to his group by Campbell himself, upon hiring.

Fletcher popped to his feet, and rushed to the window, inadvertently tearing the blinds off.

The container remained in place, blotting out the compound's lights. Their quarters were doused in dark, save for a slight glow oozing around the container and its forklift's reach.

He couldn't grasp the reality of what he saw.

Bipedal lizards atop the other two trailers. One on the building directly next to theirs, a space of no more than fifteen feet between. And two on the farthest. Too big to be mutants. His mind processed what they were, but that was impossible.

Wasn't it?

One of their pointed heads turned toward him, and he ducked. Back to the wall, muttering to himself inaudibly. His eyes darted around.

"What?" Armijo asked in a harsh whisper. "What is it?"

Above them, tapping. Something sharp against the trailer's roof. And then footsteps. Creaking.

Armijo's brow furrowed as he looked up, squatting low. Then he glanced back at Fletcher. The man was shaking his head, eyes shut, and mouthing words he couldn't make out.

"Fletcher, goddammit!" Armijo snapped, under his breath.

Fletcher's dim blue eyes shot open.

Just then a trilling from the far trailer. Screams. Armijo's own men. No gunfire. Just shrieks that weren't human, and shrieks that were.

Armijo's mind raced, recalling what the woman had said. Reading Fletcher's shock. And the sounds. And then a new one above them. Snorting.

"No," he muttered.

Jordan Labella screamed behind the bathroom door. Part of it had broken against the reptilian snout of his attacker. It snorted and snarled as it jabbed at him, clawed hands gripping the doorjambs for leverage.

Behind the creature's stiff, long tail, Channing Harbison counted his blessings—

And then charged it from across the trailer.

He had to run directly beneath the gaping, jagged hole in the ceiling, through which another of the creatures snapped its jaws but did not descend.

Harbison side-stepped the long reptilian tail and plunged his knife into its right haunch. The creature shrieked and withdrew from the partially broken bathroom door, giving the half-naked Labella a chance.

It turned and snarled at Harbison.

He looked it in the eye, both of them, set on either side of its skull and yet able to peer forward. Split pupils in a sea of amber. Pebbled, scaly skin in shades of green, from bright to dark.

The creature was about eight feet long, five at the

shoulder.

Despite being several inches shorter than either of the men, its size was still imposing. Its other features contributed to the terror it induced.

Harbison gulped, wielding his knife, shocked he was able to stab and withdraw it in the same motion, before the thing turned on him. Otherwise it would have surely broken his arm in the process. The creature was huge; larger than any lizard should be. Yet it had a bird-like stance that Harbison couldn't ignore.

His brain told him what it was.

He had seen enough movies and children's books. The latter depicted them feathered and vibrant. Almost cartoonish.

This was neither.

Its colors in the dark trailer were null and void. Its yellow-orange eyes seeming to pulse like beacons of hunger.

Harbison watched its stiff, coarse lips vibrate as it snarled, jaws barely ajar. He glimpsed the shimmer of salivated teeth, slightly curved and absurdly sharp.

A thick, pink tongue lifted within the cage of fangs, heralding a louder sound.

Labella's towel was around his waist when he lunged at the raptor's hindquarters. The giant shard of wood in his hands was like a sword of splinters. Several gave way in his callused palms, but he barely noticed. The adrenaline fueled him the rest of the way. The sharp wooden tip dug into the raptor's flesh, but it might not have punctured its hide alone.

Which was why Labella aimed for the glistening red

spot on its right hip. Where his friend and comrade had stabbed it. Now he twisted the shard of wood, and screamed a sort of war-cry of strain as he accepted the splinters as consequence.

The creature's head whipped back, shrieking. Its tail swung, violently, striking Labella and knocking him over. He let go of the two-foot sword of wood, his own hands bleeding. It protruded from the raptor's hip, at least six inches of its tapered end dug in.

Above and behind Harbison, the other raptor snapped at the pieces of the roof keeping its large frame from safely descending. Somehow, its smaller cohort had fallen through the trailer roof instead of itself.

Harbison yelled and lunged at the wounded raptor before him, just as it turned to swipe at the piece of wood with one of its clawed hands. Instead of going for a slicing maneuver, Harbison punctuated his momentum with a stabbing motion. The bloodied blade cut into the raptor's left shoulder, and it immediately faced him, hissing. Teeth grazed Harbison's face, drawing blood from his left cheek. He staggered back, releasing the knife, and careened into a table.

"Watch out!" Labella, scrambling to his feet, screamed.

Harbison looked up. The larger of the two creatures descended through the roof with a crash. It landed awkwardly, hissing and snapping out at Harbison. He ran past it, flinging the table in his wake. The giant brown-skinned raptor bent the metal card table with its jaws alone. Harbison stumbled toward the door, joining Labella as they emerged onto the rickety wooden stoop.

"How?" Harbison asked, brow furrowed. He was looking down at Labella, the man's dark skin still slick from the shower. Moreover, his white towel remained secured around his waist.

"One miracle at a time, baby," he shrugged, and then they remembered the harsh reality of the situation.

A hissing snarl erupted behind them.

Harbison slammed the door shut and followed Labella down the steps. Leaping two at a time and finding their bare feet on raw dirt. It was remotely moist, from the rain that had graced the region two days ago.

Clad in no more than a white undershirt and black briefs, Harbison felt almost as naked—given the circumstances—as Labella.

They heard screams and shouting, shrieking and trilling, from the other two trailers. Theirs was the farthest from Armijo and Fletcher's.

Labella had reached the end of the middle trailer when he froze. Harbison looked up, seeing nothing on top of the middle trailer. He glanced back at theirs, knowing that at any second the larger of the creatures would burst through that door. Sure, it was metal, and thick, but the *immensity* of that thing—

Harbison's progress halted as he bumped into the inert Labella. His feet smacked the ground and he faced forward, past Labella's right shoulder.

Between them and the outhouses stood another of those creatures, this one almost as big as the one back in their trailer. It was much more colorful, though. The arrangement of greens and browns still wasn't as vibrant as the "smaller" raptor that had attacked Labella fresh out of the shower. This one's sheer brute size was too terrifying to even acknowledge the beauty it might possess in better lighting.

It seemed unaware of their existence, though.

Kilo looked around, observing cylindrical structures in front of it. Two of them, each a little larger than a human. Inanimate, though. Neither threat nor food. Its nostrils flared, snorting in sharp and deep breaths.

There was a lot to take in, here.

The scents from the two small structures were powerful and rancid. It looked away, toward what appeared to be an opening in the towering wall surrounding this place.

Meanwhile, his companions hissed and trilled with aggression. Not at him, but their prey. Kilo couldn't grasp what this place was, except for maybe a new pen. To make up for their sparse meal hours ago. This pen had no vegetation, just containers with food in them.

Kilo strode toward the opening in the wall.

Negative. Not a complete opening. A gate of some kind, resemblant of the one that had kept them in that solid cage, the one that brought them here. A higher leap than any of them would have liked. More than their ten-foot verticals.

Or fifteen, for Hestia.

Kilo could almost make that, but even with his muscled legs he couldn't leap higher than thirteen, and that was pushing it.

He snorted as he raked in the air slightly fresher on the other side of the gate. Slightly cleaner and less rank.

The gate's bars were thick and unyielding, the spaces between not slim enough for even the leanest of them to squeeze through.

On that note, he wondered how Victor was doing. The smallest of them, though not by far. He and Six were slender killing machines. Horace longer by half a foot. Scar by another. Kilo and Hestia far more.

Even so, Victor and Six were forces to be reckoned with in the company of humans. Especially now, given a form of freedom.

Suddenly one of the others let out a choppy sound. Between a bark and a squawk. It repeated four times.

Kilo hissed and turned away from the gate, leaping onto the roof of the nearest structure, where Six was prowling. Taking his time, before now. He joined Kilo in reuniting with Victor and Scar, the latter of whom had apparently tried to enter the middle structure through a small opening. It had shattered, and likely scarred him even further.

Scar's feet anchored against the exterior wall, claws scoring the material.

He tried to pull himself free, while within, two humans struck him with blunt objects. Nothing sharp. Just their voices, and inanimate weapons.

Victor leapt from the wooden stoop and collided with Scar's hindquarters, knocking him free. Violently. The window frame crunched, and glass came away in shards, one stuck into his neck. He hissed and chirruped, legs kicking on the ground until he flipped himself over.

Victor got to his feet, too, only to be snapped at by Scar. They quarreled, dealing no more than nips at each other's tough hide.

Kilo, atop the nearest structure and beside an alerted Six, roared. The two raptors' attention was seized. They looked up. Just then the glass shard stuck in Scar's neck was knocked loose by Victor's snout.

Scar gave him a little bit of attitude but it was fleeting. He was grateful.

The sound of Hestia breaking loose of the far structure, its wooden stoop destabilizing beneath her, redirected their attention. Now *she* squawked, calling them. They came running, clawed feet kicking up moist dirt in their wake.

Horace joined her outside. She licked his wound, a deep puncture in his hip. He flinched but didn't retaliate. He was tenfold as grateful as Scar was for Victor.

Hestia didn't persist for long, though.

She snorted at Victor and Six. They tended to Horace. Victor even brushed snouts with Horace, a transient greeting. Or a distraction as Six picked splinters from Horace's wound with his teeth.

Horace whimpered softly.

Even the weakest of them needed care.

Especially if they were to make it out of here, together no less.

Odds increased in numbers.

The scent of their prey was still in the air, particularly in the olfactory senses of Hestia and Kilo. Horace's were jarred by the collisions with his snout earlier, the breaking of a door not to mention when he crashed through the roof of a structure.

Now Hestia and Kilo brushed sides as they peered

up, studying the high walls surrounding this new pen of theirs. Solid to the very top, unlike their last prison. No sharp wire, no corded fencing and inward posts.

Hestia wondered if touching the wall would cause jolts of pain like the others.

She snorted at Kilo, and he went off to check.

When she looked at Scar, he was already trotting off. Not to investigate their containment. To hunt.

Two mornings ago, Josh Guidry was kissing his youngest son on the forehead and telling his fiancé he would be back at the end of the week. Promising them both that they would catch a little R&R together.

Neither he nor David Hsu could have predicted that in two days' time, they would be frantically bludgeoning a dinosaur in the face with a table and chair.

Now, they sat with their backs against the wall opposite the window through with the creature had crashed, catching their breaths.

"Whatever you do," Hsu said. "Do not tell Fletcher…that we…wished we had knives."

"But…we do."

"Be that as it may," Hsu shook his head. They spoke quietly. "He won't ever…shut up about it."

"True," Guidry nodded.

They paused, focused on their breathing. It wasn't about exertion, it was the sheer fact of what had just happened. The flabbergasting reality.

And that they survived by using objects in the trailer.

"Supposing we're alive long enough to have any

form of conversation," Guidry added.

"Shut up. You're gonna make it back to Lauren. And your boy. What's his name again? Lauren's son. Ah, yes. Lauren."

Guidry smirked and shook his head.

"You asshole."

Hsu got to his feet, but stayed low. Away from the shattered window's line of sight. He hobbled toward his bed, and fished out a flashlight in a bag beside it. Then he returned to Guidry, who had crawled toward his own and retrieved one, too. They were pen flashlights that most of the men carried.

"Hey," Hsu said, grabbing Guidry's shoulder. His expression and voice solemn. "You're gonna see them again. Lauren and Cody. We're gonna make damn sure of it."

Guidry nodded, gulping.

"And you're gonna see…whatever Puerto Rican you're dating right now."

Hsu smirked. "I appreciate you looking out for me and Ana."

"Always, bud," Guidry said, mustering his own smile. Their cushiony humor was short-lived, deflated when a heavy weight slammed into the door fifteen feet in front of them. The metal slab clanged, the handle rattling in its socket. Another impact and the hinges jittered in place.

"Fuck, it's back," Hsu mumbled.

"We need to get outta here. Fish in a barrel."

Hsu shook his head and rushed to the window. He and Guidry had not gotten a chance to throw on their boots and remained in their snug sleepwear. Guidry wore socks and Hsu was barefoot. He paused at the edge of where glass fragments littered the carpet.

"Dammit, man," Guidry said under his breath, cringing as he watched Hsu stand less than ten feet to the left of the door.

And then Hsu raised his flashlight and thumbed the button on the end, repeatedly. Rhythmically.

The beam passed through the blinds in the foremost trailer. Catching the window, the glass intact unlike the one before Hsu.

Meanwhile, the door to his right threatened to break in. The slab wouldn't do more than warp, but the knob and deadbolt were bound to give way before the hinges. At any rate, the raptor on the other side had maybe two or three more impacts before it gained admission.

Guidry watched, chewing his lip, unsure how to proceed if—when—the dinosaur burst in.

"C'mon, c'mon," Hsu muttered, continuing with the flashlight.

Harbison slapped Labella's shoulder, and then tugged on his arm. They battled their overlapping fear until one or the other chose to move. They had since circumvented the end of their trailer, and reached the left side of the middle one. Now they faced the side of the walled-off area opposite where the outhouses were.

They went from watching the large green and brown raptor stare at the outhouses to head toward the gate, and then they withdrew, behind their trailer to head toward the other end. They were three trailers from Armijo and

Fletcher, whose condition they worriedly questioned.

Now they watched that same damn creature nudge and sniff the perimeter wall thirty feet away.

As if testing it.

The raptor was enormous. Ten feet long, six at the shoulder. Fully upright, its skull would hover off the ground inches above theirs.

To face such a beast nose-to-nose would mean certain death. Especially defenseless.

That they had survived what they did back in their trailer was an overt blessing itself.

Now they were out in the open, more or less, and not liking it. Their progress toward the others was suddenly relented. Should they retreat behind the middle trailer, and return to theirs? Or advance, and risk being spotted?

Labella somehow leading, made the decision to push forward. It was only two or three long strides before his bare feet slid to the right, back hugging the wall of the middle trailer, until he and Harbison turned the corner.

Out of sight from the large raptor sniffing the perimeter wall, the two men caught their breaths.

Relief was fleeting.

To their far right was the wooden stoop of Hsu and Guidry's trailer, crumbled and in pieces. Leaping over it, and slamming its head into the door, was yet another creature. It had small cuts in its neck, and its snout had seen better days.

Harbison gawked in fear, dreading the safety and condition of his two friends and comrades inside.

Beside the crushed stoop were several pieces of glass. The window above had been shattered, and then some. Its entire frame partially destroyed, claw marks arraying the wall around it.

Then Labella saw it, a second or two before Harbison noticed the flashing beam.

Except Labella saw what Harbison didn't—where the light made contact. The outside of the first trailer's window.

"Morse," Labella whispered. "It's Hsu or Guidry. They're trying to contact the others."

Armijo and Fletcher were in the trailer that was now in front of them. They could only hope that the two men were still alive, whether or not still inside.

Labella and Harbison had their doubts, but they were outweighed by faith. In Armijo and Fletcher as soldiers, survivors, and fighters in more than one capacity. They had been friends for longer than any of the men, through boot and then overseas.

It was reasonable to believe that if either of the two faced death, the other would give his to save him. Even if the odds were unfavorable.

And they would not be quiet about it.

No dinosaur could overpower that sound.

<u>5</u>

Too quiet. The only noise they could hear came from the trailer behind them. Something heavy and blunt slamming against metal. Joined by a series of sibilating grunts. Through the window beside their door Armijo could see that the gate and outhouses were devoid of activity. He even spotted faint footprints in the wet dirt, from the outhouses to the gate, of a large raptor.

A fucking *dinosaur*.

Armijo had since accepted the terrifying reality. He had caught glimpses through windows, he and Fletcher too wary of being seen to actually observe for longer than a second each time.

Only now they were witness to the more undeniable reality. A flashlight beam flickering through the window closest to Armijo's bed caught their attention. Peeking through the base of the pane, facing the middle trailer, the two men saw one of the creatures head-butting its door. The crushed wooden stoop beneath it.

And there, to the right of the door, Hsu in the window. His flashlight beam blinking a message in Morse. Before the men made it to their own window, Armijo and Fletcher deduced the SOS.

"We, uh, we need to get its attention," Armijo said, his mind racing.

They were grateful that the creature previously on top of their trailer had since departed. Judging from what they could see versus what they could not, they presumed the others—how many, exactly, they couldn't fathom—were on the far side of the quarters.

Either between the other two trailers or on the opposite side of Labella and Harbison's.

They tried to keep their minds from wallowing in fear for their friends.

Suddenly the door gave way, deadbolt ripping through the jamb. The metal slab swung into the trailer, splinters of wood flying.

Inside, Hsu screamed and staggered.

The raptor grunted and hoisted itself through the doorway, its haunches squeezing past the frame. It snarled at Guidry, back to the opposite wall, but Hsu's movement drew its attention. Its head jerked to the right, and the creature hissed before attacking, three-fingered hands spreading.

Guidry got to his feet to help, or to distract the creature.

Hsu could not get away.

The raptor's jaws latched onto his right shoulder, teeth digging through flesh, muscle, and snagging bone. He screamed and was pulled back, unable to look his attacker in the eye. Clawed hands gripped his waist, curved tips puncturing the meat of his body just as easily as his fitted undershirt. A lung was hooked and began to fill. Hsu regurgitated blood, before proceeding to choke on it.

The raptor's one scarred eye had not impaired its vision enough to keep it from seizing Hsu.

Behind it, Guidry shouted and tried leaping onto the creature. Its wriggling hindquarters and stiff tail flung him off. The back of his head struck the window beneath which he and Hsu had previously been cowering. The glass splintered and his eyes fluttered.

Consciousness did not entirely evade him, but clarity did.

Outside, Labella and Harbison no longer stood still as statues. They had advanced toward the door, intent on helping. They even glimpsed Armijo and Fletcher through their window, above and behind them. They had lifted the pane, and prepared to shout in hopes of catching the creature's attention.

Connecting gazes with them, it was apparent Labella and Harbison needed to act.

They exchanged glances, nods, and then Labella charged ahead.

Harbison paused not out of fear, but in thought. He recalled Labella's family, their love for him and his for them. He recalled his own estranged wife, and a son who wanted nothing to do with him. The drunken episodes of his past, despite Harbison's years of service and ongoing 560 days of sobriety.

He knew he would not live to see 561.

Harbison ran toward the trailer, scooping up a ten-inch shard of glass from the dirt, shouting simultaneously. Labella had just reached the stoop ruins, bending over to retrieve a stake of wood. He looked, distracted by the sound, and Harbison knocked him over.

"What the hell are you—!?" Fletcher started to exclaim.

Harbison threw himself into the trailer, leaping more than climbing, cutting his arm and knee in the process. He tumbled across the trailer floor, blood smearing the already tarnished carpet. From his arm, knee, and the hand gripping the piece of glass.

The raptor to his right had dropped Hsu to his stomach, and begun chewing through the back of his skull. Harbison's snarling and grunting caught its attention, turning the raptor away from its kill.

Guidry was borderline catatonic, bound to be the raptor's next victim.

Before it could turn completely, Harbison lunged at the creature from his knees, swiping the shard of glass across its left heel. The creature cried out and staggered, limping.

"Guidry! Josh!" Harbison shouted, on his stomach. "Get up, get the fuck up!"

Outside of the trailer, Fletcher had dismissed Armijo's warnings and ran for the front door. He wanted to join, to help. He had flung his door open just in time for Armijo to tackle him. The door shut again, and Fletcher wrestled against him.

"For fuck's sake, *stop*!" Armijo demanded, putting his own best friend in a headlock. Armijo spoke aggressively, but under his breath. "The others are coming! It's too many!"

Armijo had heard the heavy breaths and wet footfalls of the other raptors approach from the far side of the quarters, before colliding with Fletcher.

Outside their trailer, between it and Guidry's, Labella's eyes widened. Raptors flanked both sides of him, forcing Labella's heart into his throat.

They paused for half a second to assess their prey before shrieking, fingers spread and jaws darting forward. Then their bodies. The avian reptiles charged, two on either side of him.

Labella dropped to the dirt and rolled under the trailer, a space so tight his broad shoulders were barely able to make it. Had he worn any clothes or gear, it would have been problematic.

Jaws snapped after him, two of the smaller raptors kneeling and forcing their heads, arms, and shoulders under the building. Labella screamed through a weeping sound, lamenting the sacrifice that Harbison had made, unbeknownst of his exact condition. Ironically, he knew Harbison was somewhere directly above him, separated by only a few feet of wood, insulation, and carpet.

The two raptors were hopeless at squeezing into the gap, their haunches far too wide. Even when another skirted around to the backside of the trailer to attempt reaching Labella that way. It forced him to roll away from that edge, and curl into the fetal position in nothing but his towel, in the mud, the underbelly of the trailer millimeters above him.

Inside the building, Harbison crawled toward Guidry. He shook his shoulders repeatedly, and then slapped him with his free hand. The other still clutched the piece of glass, now bloody on both ends.

Guidry's eyes began to open, clarity returning to him. As it did, the sight of the scar-faced raptor looming over Harbison stole the scream from his lungs.

Its jaws snapped down, teeth locking onto Harbison's skull, puncturing brow and nape. The creature hissed, Harbison's blood frothing through its mouth, and then its head jerked up, peeling back the top half of the his skull like a can opener. Brain matter and blood splashed Guidry. The creature stepped back, its ankle wound not as severe as it initially seemed.

Guidry watched in awe, which temporarily conquered his nausea, as the raptor drank his friend's brain slop before gnashing to pieces the top half of the skull, from hair to scalp to underlying tissue. Ultimately it regurgitated some of the bone, shaking its head slightly, like a dog not entirely agreeing with what it tried to eat off the floor.

Hestia squawked at her cohorts, beckoning them out from under the structure. The human beneath it wasn't worth their trouble. If food was what they sought, and their bodies did ache for more nourishment than their last inadequate meal, her senses detected freshly spilled blood *inside* the structure. She could also discern another raptor, Scar, in its presence.

Freedom superseded feeding, though.

At least in Hestia's mind.

Victor and Six withdrew from the front gap beneath the structure, snorting with disappointment as they did. Neither Hestia nor Kilo would even attempt such an effort, as they were far too large.

Horace, meanwhile, retreated from the other side of the building, limping back to rejoin to group.

Hestia squawked a few more times, luring Scar out

of the structure, albeit tentatively. He turned his tail on the other human, presuming it to be dead due to its unresponsiveness.

No threat meant no need to kill.

Although for Scar, the *desire* remained.

Instead, he gave Hestia his full attention, standing there in the partially destroyed, open doorway. It made him a few feet higher than the others, a pretense of superiority that he didn't mind.

Hestia thought nothing of it, knowing she could make Scar submit in a matter of seconds if the need arose.

She proceeded to snort and chitter, her snout whipping up intermittently. Not at the sky, but the walls surrounding them. They were tall, sure. But from the top of a structure? That distance was almost halved.

Freedom awaited them, on the other side.

Could they not see that?

Kilo was ready. He snarled at Scar, who had started to turn in avoidance. Scar paused and hopped down from the doorway. His clawed feet smacked the wet dirt, across from the destroyed stoop. He hissed back at Kilo, but when the larger raptor slung his head into Scar, with enough force to knock him off his feet—

Scar managed to save his balance, though—

Hestia got her respect.

She nodded at Kilo, in gratitude. He simply snorted, and turned to leap onto the roof of the structure. Meanwhile, Horace's eyes shifted from Kilo to Hestia, and back again. He wasn't pleased. There was a speck of jealousy there.

Scar, despite pausing to shove his snout into the gap

between the structure and ground, simply to snort at the hiding human, wasn't the last to jump up.

Horace's hip wound impaired his vertical. Which already wasn't that impressive.

The cut on Scar's heel had been startling when it occurred, but not crippling. And his attacker's brains had been a unique flavor that he hoped to enjoy again sometime.

Sooner the better.

He and the others were still terribly famished. That sheep had been enough to satiate the smallest of them, at best, and that was if only they ate it. But it had been shared between them, torn asunder and distributed among six stomachs.

It hadn't just been insufficient.

It was torturous.

Which was why Scar initially insisted they stay and hunt down the other humans. He wasn't foolish enough to be oblivious to the potential risk, though. Somehow two of them had managed to be wounded, albeit minimally, by the humans. They had proven more resourceful and tenacious than expected.

But Scar remembered.

The humans outside of their cage, whenever he was transported from holding cell to the outdoor pen. Palpable fear; it had a scent, a flavor. Cortisol seeping through their bodies. The flinching and backpedaling.

He knew Hestia's vision of freedom had its greater benefits.

She made the first successful leap, using the edge of a structure to her advantage, for leverage. She vaulted high, but at an angle, so that her clawed feet could snag the textured surface of the wall, and help her scale. Her arms extended farther than they ever had in her life, clawed digits hooking the top ledge of the wall. She hoisted her heft up, and immediately heard a human's scream delight her earholes.

Hestia found herself perched atop the wall, its ledge two feet wide, to the left of the container. The machine supporting it began to reverse, slowly. Its motor a low hum that annoyed her. She growled and leapt on top of the container, barely making it move. Her claws tested the ribbed metallic surface for traction as the large rectangular object shifted its angle.

Behind and below, the other raptors shrieked and followed with greater zeal.

Victor and Six next. They both struggled, unable to leap as high as Hestia, but using her same method at the edge of the structure beneath them for leverage. Their lighter weight helped them scale the wall easier, although there was a fleeting moment of panic that they might fall.

Such a drop would surely kill or severely incapacitate them.

With invigorating success, Victor and Six reached the top of the wall. Six risked leaping directly for the cage framing the operator of the machine, who frantically withdrew the container from the wall. His reptilian limbs scrambled but he clung on, hissing and snapping at the man inside.

His screams filled the air.

Victor bounded on top of the container to join Hestia, although she wasn't necessarily pleased by this.

She nipped at him, snarling, and he dismounted from the container, joining Six on top of the operator cage. They briefly forgot about the man below, nudging each other with their snouts.

Meanwhile, Kilo and Scar hissed at one another, competing for who went next. Originally Hestia's idea was debatable, but now they couldn't wait. Bearing witness to the triumph of the others, they couldn't contain their excitement.

Horace was the only one that paused.

Hestia's advancement, and thus distance, was his sole motivation.

Especially when he watched Scar struggle, after Kilo made the jump first. Despite his size, Kilo's legs were muscular and his vertical impressive. He had just finished hoisting himself up onto the ledge when Scar followed, fortunately a few feet to his right. Kilo didn't teeter for long, leaping for the container itself, which had since withdrawn significantly from the wall.

He landed inside, claws scoring the already scratched padded floor.

Outside, the operator from the machine screamed again as he fumbled between the controls and his radio. Six resumed terrorizing him, Victor joining from the other side. Their jaws snapping, saliva spraying his face from above, and although neither could get to him inside, not from their angles, the man's panic overrode his other senses.

He dove from the machine, tumbling to the ground. He looked up, across the lawn, the compound's exterior lights like beacons of hope.

The massive building was only about thirty yards away. Its size made that distance seem like nothing.

It *was* nothing, right?

Reachable.

He scrambled to his feet to run.

Behind him, Victor alighted from above. It was a hollow thump, succeeded by the ripping of grass and soil beneath clawed toes that ought to be fossils.

And nothing more.

But Victor's creators had insisted.

He was their first triumph.

He wouldn't disappoint his Maker. He pursued the fleeing human, whose sloppy evasion was crippled by terror. An unprecedented fear infected with regret and guilt. For this, and everything throughout the four decades of his life.

Far back, Hestia and Six dismounted, simultaneously. Then Kilo, seconds before Scar followed, using the open container for a lower bridge to the ground below. His passing caused the machine to roll farther from the wall, its brakes not secured and the motor idling.

By the time Scar's feet touched grass, he had a slight limp.

Horace was worse off.

Still on top of a structure, still doubting himself. Except that there was no debate left. He was alone now, all of his companions had escaped. Hestia seemed to have forgotten about him.

He called out, his squawks weak and desperate. They echoed through the open night air.

Hestia paused, sixty feet from the wall. She looked

back at it, past Scar and the machine. Its wheeled roll farther from the wall made going back a severe risk. A leap of faith not worth the struggle.

She snorted, counting her losses.

In all honesty, it wasn't much.

Horace had never been a very worthy predator, anyway.

She looked ahead.

Victor, meanwhile, was proving that size and heft was not critical to seizing prey.

His fleeing human quarry stumbled, across the width of a narrow dirt path, dust kicking up around him. Hestia knew that there was no hope for the man, even if he sprinted flawlessly. Her kind had never been clocked in the open, but she had faith that most of them could rip across a field of green—the thing of dreams—faster and nimbler than any human could.

Victor made the pounce, about twenty feet past the dirt path.

The man screamed, turning in awe to face his attacker. His wail heightened in a wavering crescendo. Victor's toe claws sunk like sickles into his thighs, claws seizing shoulders and jaws burrowing into the jugular. His body hit the ground, femurs crushing and clavicles shattering. His right carotid artery gushed warm, nectarous blood into Victor's throat.

Hestia watched his tail whip up behind him, ecstatic of the kill.

She turned and squawked at the others. Kilo joined Scar as they bounced toward her. The two males nipped at each other with a long lost sense of playfulness, Scar expressing his guilt for hesitating.

This freedom that Hestia had sought was a priceless victory.

Speaking of victors…

Hestia called the feasting raptor from afar. Victor lifted his bloodied muzzle from his kill and turned his head toward the others. A slender tongue licked gore from his lips and teeth, scratching an itch along the side of the pink muscle.

A purring sound exited his moist throat before he abandoned—temporarily, at least—his kill and rejoined the others.

That Horace wouldn't make it had been assumed, accepted, and dismissed in a span of seconds. Hestia transmitted this much in her eyes and inflection.

Now, onto more pressing matters.

The two F's. Feast and freedom.

Neither could come fast enough.

Hestia squawked at Victor and Six, gesturing her skull toward the far side of the property, opposite the walled-off area they just escaped from. A tall metallic fence topped with sharp wire that gleamed against the compound's lights curved around the perimeter.

Victor and Six nodded, turning to investigate. In passing, as they trotted off, Six licked human blood from Victor's snout. He didn't complain.

Inside the wall, Horace made the leap, following the same method as the others. The instant he applied pressure in a springing motion, an unconquerable pain stung his haunches, effort wasted. Horace met the wall seven feet short of the wall, and didn't have the strength to scale the rest of the way.

Horace fell, tumbling awkwardly.

He hit the ground, and no amount of residual moisture could have cushioned his impact.

His left tibia snapped, protruding through the flesh of his thigh. A rib cracked but missed a lung by centimeters, instead ripping into his stomach lining. His wrist broke beneath the weight of his body, ulna fractured and hand going limp.

Horace was in a mess of pain and incapacity as he wailed and writhed at the base of the wall.

Hestia and the others heard this. There was an iota of pity to be felt, but it was abandoned when a jarring sound emitted from the larger building. The horde of exterior lights shut off, and the sound ended shortly after it began.

She snorted and turned away from the others.

Her route was quickly realized by Kilo and Scar. They avidly followed.

6

Covered in mud but still gripping his towel, Jordan Labella was helped out from under the trailer by Fletcher. Armijo climbed into the building, covering his mouth at the sight of his two friends and comrades, butchered. Even the severest animal attack somehow paled in comparison to this outcome.

David Hsu on his stomach, in a carpet-soaked pool of his own blood. And Channing Harbison, on his back, his legs bent and feet inches from Guidry's. Harbison was missing the top half of his skull, his eyes still in their sockets, gawking in blank terror and pain up at the ceiling.

Armijo caught a glimpse of them and for that split-second he knew he would be haunted for the rest of his days.

Supposing he saw any after tonight.

Pitying Guidry for having witnessed even a fraction of this bloodbath unfold, much less being defenseless during it, Armijo hunkered beside him. He held the man like a shaken child.

This was fleeting.

Guidry pulled away, wobbling to his feet and staggering over the puddle of vomit he had discharged minutes ago. Only to fall to his knees, and brace himself against the bed. Elbows on the mattress, he interlocked his fingers and bowed his head.

Genuflecting, Josh Guidry was torn between praying for the sanctity of his slaughtered friends' souls and for the death of their killer. It was just an animal, right? No. It was a monster.

All of them.

In Guidry's mind, they were mindless beasts worthy of violent deaths.

"Eric," Fletcher muttered from the doorway.

Armijo turned. Fletcher cleared his throat and gathered himself.

"Are they all gone?" Armijo asked.

"All but one. Fucker didn't make the jump. Can't seem to move."

"Still alive?"

"Holding on."

Guidry shoved his way past Armijo, boots already laced up. He was still in nothing more than briefs and an undershirt, but he dismounted from the trailer, stumbling over pieces of wood, next to Fletcher. He tried to restrain Guidry, who slipped free, only to draw Fletcher's sheathed knife.

"Goddammit, Josh," Fletcher huffed under his breath, and lunged for Guidry.

The man eluded him.

Armijo dismounted from the trailer and slapped the back of Fletcher's shoulder.

They looked at each other before running after Guidry. Labella was at his heels, too. Except that Fletcher held Labella back while Armijo unsheathed his combat knife and—instead of restraining Guidry—joined him.

The crippled raptor hissed and snarled as they towered over it. The creature was on its side, bleeding from internal injuries and compound fractures.

A viciously clawed foot kicked at Armijo, but he dodged it and stomped the ankle into the ground. Crushing it beneath his boot on the second impact. The creature wailed and whipped its tail, slapping against the wet earth. A clawed hand feebly reached for Guidry.

He was under-dressed but this didn't count for much. He harbored twice, at least, the spite toward the animal than his comrades.

Armijo had only glimpsed Harbison's sacrifice, not witnessed it inches away.

He realized that Guidry's head injury had not impaired his motor functions and combat efficiency. He calculated the raptor's frantic motions and evaded them as he thrusted Fletcher's knife in a frenzy of stabbing strikes. Although frenetic himself, Guidry was able to channel it methodically, which conquered the raptor's bestial behavior.

Especially in its helplessness.

There was no pity to be had. Only the opportunity to take advantage of.

Seconds lapsed into what felt like one long, slow, brutal moment. By its end, Guidry had repeatedly stabbed the raptor in the face, neck, and shoulder with the full-tang carbon steel KA-BAR. The black blade gleamed with the crimson blood of the beast.

"Should've stayed extinct," Guidry snarled, and spit on its corpse.

He turned away, not acknowledging Armijo's assistance, and lumbered back toward the trailers. He dropped the knife at Fletcher's feet, his movement and expression aloof. Labella rushed to join him, and they circled around to enter one of the trailers. Certainly not either of theirs. They instead gathered their bearings inside Armijo and Fletcher's trailer.

Waters from the refrigerator.

Labella shed his towel in the bathroom and rinsed off, hastily.

Outside, Fletcher rejoined Armijo. The man had yet stepped away from the slain creature. He couldn't take his eyes off of it. The features, its slight avian anatomy despite the strong reptilian traits.

"This isn't right," Armijo shook his head.

"Ain't that the truth?" Fletcher said.

"No, I mean…" Armijo sighed and turned away. "This isn't *just* a…a dinosaur. I'm no paleontologist but I've seen books. Museums. It's been a while since I've been a good father, but I remember. Tony loved those things. The bright feathers, like fierce pigeons the size of a Great Dane. Not…Not *these*. These were *made* to be monsters. And set loose upon us. Like you said."

"Fish in a barrel," Fletcher muttered. He shook his head, vehemently. "No, this is fucking crazy."

A jarring alarm from the compound, over the wall. Its exterior lights shut off. The sound of raptors squawking and trilling in the silence. And then nothingness. The alarm itself had been short-lived.

"Whatever the case," Armijo sighed. "We gotta get our shit together and get the fuck outta here."

"Can't argue there."

"Have you seen the gate?" Armijo exchanged words with Fletcher en route to their trailer.

"Locked us in like cattle. A chunk of metal, but basic enough. I think I can pick it."

"With what?"

"I don't know. Something from behind the fridge. Maybe a bedspring. Or one of the hairs on your ass."

"Better off plucking one of those grays from your beard, old man."

"Hey, at least I can grow one," Fletcher scratched his hairy neck.

"It's a work-in-progress, fuck-face." Armijo jeered, rubbing his goatee.

They returned to their trailer. Upon reentrance, they were relieved to see Labella cleaned up. He walked past them, naked head to toe.

"We've got more important things to do, ladies," he said in passing. "So stop staring and get to work."

"Psh," Fletcher rolled his eyes.

Armijo tried to smirk. Labella exited the trailer and jogged across the quarters toward his and Harbison's. It was a struggle not to let consciousness slip from his grasp and the weakness of grief hit him like a locomotive when he returned to it. His bunkmate's corpse was in another building, but still.

He recalled everything, from Harbison's shoving of Labella to his actual aggressive sacrifice, saving Guidry's life. To Labella's own retreat beneath the trailer, and all that followed. The sounds, the hissing and snorting and snarling. Vulture-like squawking, avian steps and talons, wielded like predatorial lizards.

It was some kind of twisted nightmare.

He finally managed to gather his bearings after vomiting in the toilet. He washed his face and proceeded to get dressed without looking at himself in the mirror. He couldn't bear to.

He wondered if that day might ever come.

And what his family would think, knowing the truth. Or did they need to?

First he would actually have to make it back to them. And give what Harbison had surrendered some value.

So Labella got dressed, urgently.

Meanwhile, Armijo joined Fletcher by the gate. A bedspring had proven more useful than previously anticipated, and Armijo owed his friend a small apology for underestimating his capabilities with so little.

This might have otherwise triggered a crude joke, but their minds had tunnel-vision. There was an objective and that was escape first, then reach the compound. They needed their weapons if they were going to survive a single minute outside these walls.

At the absolute least, the guns would comfort them. Before they left, however, not a single one of them was without a combat knife. Although Guidry had not brought his own, Labella had excavated the late Harbison's for him to carry.

Guidry touched the pommel to his forehead and Labella watched a silent prayer sneak past his lips.

And then they were ready.

Or as ready as the men could be, given their circumstances.

The lock came undone, chains rattling against the steel gate loudly. The men cringed as they pushed the heavy gates open, hinges creaking, and cautiously emerged from their quarters.

A mere three or four steps and they froze.

Fletcher indicated a pair of raptors about fifty yards to their right, just past a small knoll, repeatedly probing the electrified perimeter fence.

The periodic shocks sparked light into the darkness, and made the raptors hiss and shriek, shaking their snouts before proceeding down the length of the fence.

It was a relief they took advantage of, and moved left. Until their backs were to the outer wall, facing the compound, and more directly the parking garage a little over one-hundred yards away. The length of a football field, to sprint in the open, exposed and easily attacked, should there be other raptors lurking.

With the compound's exterior lights turned off, it was difficult to discern much in the darkness.

The lamps illuminating the parking garage, on the other side of the narrow, hairpin access road, were the only other source of light they could see. It was two levels, but nobody ever parked up top. The concrete cover was primarily for shelter during harsh weather.

Armijo noticed, even from this range, that less than half of the vehicles remained. Which meant that the compound was running on a skeleton crew of sorts. And if the raptors got inside, that would be literal in under an hour.

Unless Campbell's on-site security team were more

attuned to the situation than Bravo had been.

Left completely in the dark, about everything.

Armijo hated to work it over in his head this way, but he had begun to fear what seemed obvious at this point—

"We were *hired* to be a *test*," he thought out loud, shaking his head.

"Please, Christ, don't start," Fletcher sighed. "I can't handle that shit right now."

"Even if it is what we're all thinking," Labella said, regret and disgust on his tongue. Anger seeping through.

The latter emotion, especially, had worked over Guidry's expression.

"Sorry, guys." Armijo bowed his head. He raked in a few deep breaths and then looked up. He drew his knife, gripping it firmly.

To their far left was further evidence of Armijo's previous statement. The forklift and its massive container raised, to unleash the creatures into their quarters, over the wall. The forklift had since reversed, but judging by the mutilated lump of a body fifty feet from it, on the grass just past the dirt path, its operator had not survived.

And the raptors had successfully escaped.

"What's the plan?" Labella asked.

"I say we dash for the warehouse. The access door, anyway."

The others looked at Armijo, and then each other. The plan was sound enough, and they knew his reason.

"The armory," Fletcher said. "But it's probably locked. Hell, that access door might be locked, too."

"Maybe. But worth a shot," Armijo shrugged. "Better than hauling ass to the parking garage."

"I *could* hot-wire a car," Fletcher said.

They had carpooled here two days ago, in a large truck with their gear in the bed. Only the keys had been confiscated by Campbell's security team, again, "as a precaution."

All of those conditions had started to really work their way under the men's skin the more they recalled them. Guilt of being so naïve threatened to overtake their other emotions.

"I don't doubt that," Armijo said. "But I can't help but think you wouldn't be able to outrun one of those fuckers in the open."

Fletcher looked around. He even took a few long strides away from the wall.

"I don't see any. Just the idiots back there, testing the fence."

"Which is electrified," Labella scoffed, shaking his head. "Campbell told us they weren't."

"Another lie, shocking," Guidry said, his voice droning.

Nobody was going to point out the obvious pun.

"Let's focus, gentlemen," Armijo said. "I say we book it to the warehouse door. Better chances, even if it's locked."

"And if it is?" Fletcher asked.

"We'll use your big, dumb head to break it down."

Fletcher sighed and folded. "Who's leading?"

They turned toward Labella. He scoffed.

"I hate being the fastest of you slowpokes," he said,

shaking his head.

"Are you ready for this?" Armijo asked, not just Labella but Guidry as well.

Everybody nodded. Staring at this end of the compound. They would have to cut left and sprint across the grass, toward the warehouse. It was closer than the main entrance, at least; about a forty-yard dash.

Labella led by example, abandoning his doubts and taking initiative. He didn't abandon fear as much as he did mask it with drive.

The others followed suit.

As comparably stupid and single-minded as humans were, at least to her, they surprised Hestia. The massive building appeared to be on lockdown, secured from the inside out. She and the others probed every possible opening for a way inside.

It was ultimately Kilo who found one.

Likely thanks to the sheer weight and force he was able to put behind his snout, Kilo broke the slatted covering over an air duct, and thrusted his head inside. He looked around. It was dark and bland in taste, the air crisp but sour all at once.

More than anything, the space was narrow.

Too confining for him or Hestia, or even Scar, to squeeze into.

He suddenly wished Victor and Six were with them, but had respected Hestia's decision to direct the two toward the fence.

Kilo trilled, drawing her attention.

The ventilation shaft was accessible from a low protrusion of the building, a block of concrete that likely housed some kind of ventilation unit. Next to the shaft's opening was a stiff covering, a wider space that could grant them entrance if they could open it.

She nudged it, and the metallic plate dented inward. She then hissed at Kilo, who nodded, redirecting his attention to the square. He had not noticed it earlier. He huffed and slammed the crown of his head into it. The metal dented more.

She squawked and nudged him aside with her shoulder. He growled but didn't nip at her.

Her tongue rose and fell, then she shut her jaws before jabbing at it. The metal groaned, denting, and one of the corners sprang free from the concrete.

It was nailed in place.

Hestia angled her claws, digging one under the corner, and warping it outward. Then she reeled back on her stiff tail, and kicked her right foot forward, staving the metal plate inward. It came off, crashing through a wooden slab behind it. The debris scattered across tile floor, and someone inside screamed.

The man reached for the electric baton on his hip, only to drop it in a panic as he scrambled for the door. Knocking the other man off his feet in the progress.

A weapon clattered on the tile.

Hestia stepped aside and Kilo poured in through the hole, his left leg catching on the sill. He pulled harder, and something cracked before giving way.

Alec Carter screamed as he reached the door. He pulled it

open but toilet paper caught to the sole of his boot made him slip back. His other foot slammed the door shut in the process.

Behind him, Tate Anderssen *tried* to scream. But not sound came out. It was stuck in his throat, as he rose to his elbows, having been knocked over by the frantic Carter.

Anderssen gawked as he watched the enormous raptor force itself through the previously boarded-up window. His hands fumbled for the pistol at his hip, already forgetting he had drawn it upon entering the bathroom, at the insistence of Carter.

The raptor handler heard noises outside.

With the compound on lockdown and Campbell's announcement that "the subjects had gotten loose during transit," Anderssen was one of the first to retreat from the warehouse. The farther into the building he went, the safer he felt. And the closer to the front, to the access road and ultimately the parking garage, to his car, the better.

Duty called, though.

And with a gun on his hip, he tentatively answered when Carter demanded his attention.

Now he was regretting it.

Seeing the creatures in their pens, cells, and cages was terrifying enough. This was an entirely separate nightmare.

The hefty *Deinonychus* crashed through part of the wall, gaping the no longer barricaded window further, and slid across the bathroom floor.

Anderssen whimpered as terror coursed through him. An infection he could not ignore.

He sat up, and lunged forward, hands sprawling after the pistol.

He recognized Kilo as the monstrous raptor's jaws neared. Clawed feet slipping on the tile in an attempt to hoist its body up.

Anderssen gagged on fear.

His hands wrapped around the pistol.

Behind him, Carter scampered to his feet and pulled the door open.

Kilo hissed before the sound thickened with blood, its teeth grazing Carter's jugular as he withdrew. Blood gushed across Kilo's tongue, and sprayed the white floor. Kilo stood, its tail whipping in the air, slashing a ceiling fixture and blanketing the bathroom in darkness. If it wasn't for the half-open door leading to the well-lit hallway outside, Carter crawling through the gap, Anderssen would have died in the pitch black.

He almost wished he had.

Kilo's darting yellow eyes passed over him. The creature snarled and warbled as it leapt after Carter, one of its sickle toe-claws opening Anderssen's face from nose to hairline. His head bounced back against the tile, the blood causing Kilo the slip.

Its immense body crashed through the door, just as Carter got to his feet, his screams echoing down the hallways.

There were so few people left in the compound, but three alone were on this level. They wailed in fear, hearing the raptor's distinct vocalizations. Hearing *it*, nevermind the screams of a fellow man.

Carter glanced back and witnessed Kilo gather its

footing before darting after him like a streamlined bullet of flesh and muscle.

And hunger.

So much hunger.

Hestia delighted in the sounds. She squawked after Scar, down on the ground and about forty feet away, his head raised, alerted to motion somewhere across the grass. She squawked again, but he screeched in defiance and darted away.

She hissed and dismissed him, assuming that he was reasonably distracted.

A high-voltage sizzling caught her attention.

She peered into the mostly dark room, via the opening Kilo had crashed through, and spotted a wounded human. A weapon by his feet, out of reach. The electrical baton, however, was in his left hand. He had seized it from the blood-tarnished floor. Its bulbous end sparked blue and white.

The man did not seem to know how to use the thing. He wasn't one of her handlers.

She could hear cries of pain and fear outside of the room. Down long corridors, echoing deliciously.

Adrenaline pumped through her organs. The excitement tickled her hunger, which ached for satiation. Or even a morsel of it.

Hestia pushed her body through the opening, and her right sickle claw sunk into the wounded man's left bicep. Blood sprayed free, misting her leg. His grip released the baton, and before she could seal his fate, time did. He succumbed to his injuries and the life fled from his eyes.

Hestia snorted and accepted the free meal.

Her snout stabbed down, ingesting Anderssen's face without his knowing.

7

Labella collided with the access door seconds before Guidry caught up to him. Then Fletcher and Armijo, the latter who watched their back, his knife at the ready. Except that the heavy steel door would barely budge. Labella cursed and jerked at the handle, juddering the door in its frame. They were both aware of the basic lock it functioned on.

Fletcher stepped around Guidry and punched the call button beside the door. They could hear it ring from outside.

He continued to hit it, and the men resisted screaming for help. They didn't want to alert any potential raptors in the area. Let alone those far off, testing the perimeter fence.

Armijo backed up, observing the outside of the building. He caught motion to his far right, and spotted one of the creatures dart across the grass, from the front of the compound.

His eyes widened, and he moved forward, pounding his fist against the door and shouting. His panic and sudden decision to raise his voice alarmed the others.

They began shouting, too.

Somehow Guidry had been pushed to the back. He took a big step away from the building, to get a better

83

view of the compound's front property. Cutting across the grass with very little curve to its itinerary was a raptor. Its streamlined movement was deeply unsettling, and Guidry felt chills sheet his bones.

He rushed back toward the door, banging and shouting with the others.

The door suddenly pushed out, almost knocking Fletcher over. Armijo grabbed a fistful of his vest and then flung him inside, making the man who opened the door stagger himself. And then Armijo pushed Labella in, before Guidry stumbled inside at his heels.

"Get in here!" Armijo heard Fletcher shout.

He ran in, hastily pulling the door behind him. Only it didn't shut all the way. A reptilian snout shoved its way between door and jamb, jaws snapping loudly and hissing breaths bellowing into the warehouse.

"Jesus!" The man who had opened the door exclaimed, behind the others.

Armijo was applying his full bodyweight in pulling the door shut, via its horizontal push-bar handle.

Fletcher suddenly lunged forward, wielding his knife. He sliced the creature's snout before adjusting it in his hand for a better stabbing motion. Only when he did, the raptor screeched and withdrew its head.

The door clanged shut and Armijo almost fell back. Automatically the door's internal lock secured. Armijo put his back to the jamb, and slid down into an exhausted sitting position.

Everyone began to relax, an iota's worth at most. And then the door rattled in its frame, a snorting hiss billowing against the steel from outside. This startled everyone out of their skin, and their verbal reactions transitioned to aggressive shouting.

Suddenly a gun went off.

It was in the hand of the man who had let them in. Cillian Gage, lead member of the compound's on-site security team. The pistol in his hand was returned to its hip holster.

Outside, the raptor could be heard yelping and scampering off.

Fresh relief washed over Bravo, ears ringing nonetheless, although Gage's dumbstruck reaction was one of a more steadfast unease.

"So it's true," he said, his voice dry. "They really did get loose."

"What?" Armijo said, part of his cheek raised, in tandem with an eyebrow.

Gage cleared his throat and glanced over his shoulder. The warehouse was spacious, enough to fit three shipping containers side by side. A high, hangar-like ceiling only had a few windows and was partially comforting.

"Dr. Campbell made an announcement not five minutes ago. Said the *subjects* got loose. But were contained outside."

"Loose, my ass," Fletcher said, shaking his head. He paced between Gage and Armijo. "And the only thing they're *contained in* is this whole perimeter fence. Everything else is an MRE to those things."

"How many are out there? All six?"

"You *knew* about these fucking *monsters* and you *still* let 'em take our fucking guns!?" Guidry exclaimed, and had to be restrained from assaulting Gage.

"Our NDA was a little more fucked-up than yours, yeah," Gage said, matter-of-factly. Guilt began to trickle through him. His voice broke a touch. "And our pay much higher."

"And your guns, much…*more*," Labella sneered.

"Look, my guy Ramirez is on that right now. He should be rifling through the armory as we speak."

"Finally, some good fuckin' news," Fletcher said. Though he was being honest, he also masked his resentment better than Guidry.

"And no, not six. Five, technically."

Gage squinted at Armijo. "What do you mean, *technically?*"

"Two went off to test the perimeter fence," Fletcher blurted. He was already walking away, toward the swing doors leading out of the warehouse.

"And one, we killed," Armijo brandished his knife. "Fucker crippled itself trying to jump that wall."

"Dumb animal," Guidry muttered.

"They're not *just* animals," Gage continued. He beckoned them to follow him, trailing Fletcher by a few feet. "Campbell bio-engineered them, with help, but adjusted their DNA to make them sleeker, stealthier, and, yes, scarier. Then he and his handlers mistreated them so as to…"

Gage paused about ten feet from the doors. Fletcher noticed and stopped within reach of them himself. He looked back.

After swallowing a lump of regret and shame in his throat, Gage continued.

"To enhance aggression," he said. Another long

pause, as they slowly came to terms.

He would have continued, except a series of sounds caught their attention. Two shrieks, both so parallel they almost overlapped. One evidently human; the other, not.

A burst of adrenaline jolted through Fletcher and he plowed through the double swinging doors. His boots skidded on the tile in the hall and his jaw practically hit the floor. Next came Gage, and the others rebounding off of them.

The men gawked in the worst kind of awe.

Shock seized their bodies as they beheld an immense raptor mutilate an overpowered Osvaldo Ramirez, not twenty feet away.

His pistol had never even been drawn, but the armory door hung open. So did his gut, sundered by a claw, his entrails half-in half-out. The raptor was too busy nipping at his face to notice; one of its feet crushed a clump of intestines against the floor.

Gage climbed out of his shock and screamed incoherently. He drew his pistol at the same time, the raptor's head whipping up and snarling. Blood dripped from its jaws. Gage's pistol lit up, a mess of bullets missing the large target, only two hitting their mark. The creature shrieked and turned, zipping around the far corner.

Ramirez asphyxiated on his own blood, most of his face rendering him unidentifiable. Gage dropped to his knees to attend to him, pistol still in one of his hands. The blood on the tile floor made him almost slip.

Armijo and Fletcher arrived to stand around him. Gage thrusted his pistol into one of their hands, he couldn't be sure which and didn't care. He frantically attempted to stuff Ramirez's intestines back into his body. He would have been writhing in pain if the man had any concept of it. His nerves were overridden and his oxygen supply fleeting.

Gage felt a firm hand on his shoulder, tugging him back. He almost fell over, away from Ramirez. The man was dead seconds later. Gage's hands were all shades of pink and red.

The rankness of spilt viscera, and death, filled the hallway.

Fletcher squatted beside him, and offered to return his pistol. Gage wiped his hands on his cargo pants, and then snatched the weapon. He trembled, a plethora of emotions storming inside of him.

"Ramirez," Fletcher said, his voice low and gritty. Sincere. "How long did you know him?"

Gage shook his head. "It's not that."

"What do you mean?"

Gage stood up, abruptly. He almost fell over in the process. Armijo lent a hand but Gage shook it off. He checked the pistol's chamber and then holstered it. Armijo followed him into the armory. Guidry and Labella were eager to enter, too.

Fletcher paused at the doorway, turning and glancing in both directions. His gaze hung heavy at the corner down from the armory, around which the raptor had fled.

His hand flexed around the combat knife before sheathing it. And then he shut the door behind them; it clicked, automatically securing. A keypad code would be required to open it again, from the inside or out.

"He meant," Guidry said, trying to keep his voice from shaking. Gage had refused to answer Fletcher, but now he looked over at Guidry as he spoke. "It doesn't matter if he knew him for a month or a decade. Casualties are always hard to stomach. In combat, we can, we can compartmentalize s-sometimes, and…carry on. But *this*…this isn't combat. This is something else."

Labella squeezed Guidry's shoulder. Guidry nodded, and then collapsed onto a bench beside a table.

Gage nodded before turning to face Armijo. His eyes shifted from him to Fletcher. And then the others, before returning to Armijo.

"You're, uh…Amijo, right? Aaron."

"Eric. Armijo."

"Sorry," Gage said, smirking unevenly. "I'm a little fucking shook."

"We all are," Fletcher said. "What's happening shouldn't be. Not ever."

Gage nodded. "There were six of you. Or am I crazy?"

"Copy," Armijo nodded. "We lost David Hsu and Channing Harbison."

Gage shook his head.

"I'm afraid they got my other guy, too. If there are any number of those things loose in the compound, the only firepower was between me, Ramirez, and Anderssen. But I haven't heard from him in a while."

Gage clenched his jaw and stared off blankly.

He didn't need to say anything for the men of Bravo to realize that this particular comrade of Gage was in fact a longtime friend. Which made it harder.

"We'll find him, one way or another, and we'll kill these fucking things," Guidry stepped forward.

Cillian Gage nodded, clearing his throat. He yanked a shotgun off its rack on the pegboard wall. And then handed the Remington Model 870 to Guidry.

"Twelve-gauge, eight-round. Remy pumps are all we got."

"Better than this," Guidry brandished a knife.

They went around, confirming names, as their hands and pockets substantiated with firepower and ammunition.

"It's too fuckin' quiet," Labella said, looking up and shaking his head.

"No, that's this room. I heard a ruckus of screams earlier, though faint, down in the warehouse." Gage pointed at the door. "Place is sealed tight. There could be a gunfight down the hall, we wouldn't hear shit."

"That's…kind of comforting."

"If we were the stay-and-wait-this-shit-out kind of guys, yeah."

"So…they're dinosaurs, right?" Fletcher asked, his voice thick, trying to force it out.

Gage sighed and walked toward the door. His fingertip hovered over the keypad. He saw how partially dried blood had framed his nail. It was Ramirez. Ramirez was still *on him*.

"What kind?" Armijo asked, noticing the look on Gage's face. Not caring to ask many questions, but knowing it would help.

"Uh," Gage started, and cleared his throat. "Raptors. Die, uh…*Deinonychus*. Hyper-intelligent pack-hunters."

"Comforting," Fletcher muttered, behind Armijo.

"Oh," Gage said, aggressively jabbing the code. "But that's not all."

Kilo licked his lips as he maneuvered the halls of the lower level. He paused to tilt his head back, eyes squinting against the fluorescent fixture inches from his snout. His tongue curled, threading his teeth and gifting his throat with the scraps.

He relished the flavor.

It was one he had not tasted in a long time, before tonight. He had forgotten how delicious it could be. Not every part of a human was a delicacy, but after being damn near starved the whole day, he didn't have the right to be picky.

Screams scattered throughout the structure on levels above him. He smiled slightly, joyed that Hestia was having her fill.

The contentment was passing, though.

Kilo hurt in a couple of places. Something burned in his right shoulder, above his arm, but not enough to impair movement. A similar pain throbbed softly on his right hip; he glanced at it. A projectile had grazed the meat, leaving a shallow trench of blood in his hide.

Kilo snorted, agitated more than anything.

As ambrosial as human flesh was, their blood like a revitalizing juice to his own organs, Kilo wasn't short-sighted. Unlike Scar. No, he knew this changed things significantly. Human projectile weapons meant that he would have to play his cards better. No more rushing his prey.

His sheer size in these comparably narrow corridors made stealth seem impractical. But not impossible.

Especially with how feeble the human mind was, in the face of fear.

He purred, looking forward to relay this new information to Hestia the best he could.

8

Trepidation imprisoned her. Not only in the bathroom stall, but within the confines of her own body. Although she shook, it was almost without motion. She didn't want to make a sound. Didn't want to alert the predators of her position. Even if they were far away, down networks of hallways preying on more exposed, frantic, and vocal targets.

She clutched her phone close, despite acknowledging its sudden uselessness. She had to hope that the one call she had gotten out was not fruitless. She had to hope that the men of Bravo were still alive, and safe.

Even if she and everyone else in the compound weren't.

Ida Salanueva couldn't help but wonder if she and the others deserved this. The bitterness inside of her sided with the brutality of justice. That painful fates awaited Dr. Campbell, Isaacs, and even those who were casually complicit, like Janice.

Whether it be chalked up as karma or something less poetic, she didn't care.

But if that was the case, then what would spare her? That she said no and tried to be a whistleblower?

Life didn't work out like that.

She feared she would get hers, too.

The only question was…how long would Ida hide? How long could she stomach being a coward?

She wanted to be brave, to will herself to try escaping. She had her keys on her, but so what? The parking garage was down two levels, and on the opposite end of the damn building.

The irony was that this place used to be a hospital of some kind. Now it was a buffet line for some of the fiercest predators to ever live. Only made worse. *Made.*

By men—and women—who could not see past their own fame, and the milestones in scientific achievements.

That they could, had surpassed the thought that they ever *should.*

Ida wondered if the type of hospital this had once been was in fact an asylum for mental patients. That would certainly be a more appropriate irony.

She finally braved herself to lower her feet from the edge of the toilet to the floor. She initially lifted them for fear of someone entering, looking for her, and peering under the stalls. But since then, she simply clutched her shins and sobbed into her knees.

Her shoes touched the tile floor.

The door to the bathroom pushed open. She gasped, but fortunately stowed most of her breath in her throat. A hand impulsively covered her mouth, and she returned her feet to the edge of the toilet.

And then the door began to close.

She could hear its hinges creak.

Her brow furrowed, and suddenly the door pushed open again, but harder. Whatever had struck it did not relent the second time. The door cracked against the wall behind it. Footfalls proceeded, carrying the person farther inside.

A stink filled the bathroom.

Heavy, guttural breaths.

Something wet dappling the floor.

Saliva? Or blood.

Likely both.

Ida's eyes widened. It was not a person. The intruder was something far worse than even the most threatening man.

She had never seen one of the subjects outside of their holding pen. Had never looked upon it as more than something to be studied, mostly on a cellular level. She was not an animal behaviorist, but she had on more than one occasion found herself studying the creatures as such.

Ida never once saw one of the *Deinonychus* in its holding cell. She feared that the Doctor had instructed their handlers to mistreat them deliberately. It would certainly account for their heightened aggression over the last several months.

And the periodic confinement.

The fasting.

Her eyes tried to squint past the tears.

The animals had been borderline starved this evening. No wonder they hungered so much. And the maltreatment only made it worse.

As if the creatures weren't dangerous enough.

One step after another, the creature proceeded into the bathroom. It was not a large space. If two of the bigger ones occupied it at the same time, they would not be able to turn around without bumping into each other; Ida imagined their long, stiff tails slamming into the stalls, knocking off the mirrors above the sinks—

A heavy, deep, snorting breath startled her.

She had not relented her hand clasped over her mouth. Only it made the breath from her flaring nostrils seem outrageously loud. Likely more than they really were. But to a mistreated, malnourished *Deinonychus* engineered to be deadlier than its extinct counterpart?

Ida felt dizzy with fear.

The raptor shrieked before slamming a stall door open. It was the first of three, and she was in the third, farthest from it.

But not nearly far enough.

The stall door clanged and the raptor took another step. It purred a low sound, but not one of contentment.

Ida literally bit her hand, to keep herself from making a peep. Even if she was fated to die.

The raptor stepped before the second stall, its toe claw tapping the tile. Rhythmic with its patience. And then it shoved the door open, be it with the crown of its head, its snout, or possibly even its foot, she couldn't determine. The door slammed so hard the whole stall rattled. The toilet paper dispenser fell off the partition, and a roll tumbled free.

Ida could see, through the blurry vision of tears in her eyes, and the crack between her stall partition and door, the creature turn its head. It hissed, trilling a loud, piercing sound, after realizing the roll was of no interest. Then its head returned to face her stall.

It took a step.

Ida's eyelids fluttered. She was going to pass out. The apprehension alone, the anxiety of what a death from one of them must be like, was overwhelming.

The clamor of gunfire outside the bathroom, down a hall, caught the creature's attention. It snorted as it turned its large head, and then pivoted on its feet to prance toward the door. Its tail whipped the stalls as it did so, but was not gone so quickly.

It paused at the door, clawed digits curling around the door handle, a curved bar.

Hestia pulled on the apparatus as if it was wrenching something out of a wound. The door opened, just enough for her snout to fill the gap and her shoulders did the rest. She snorted as she took in the scents of the corridor again, an array of odors somehow more appetizing than the room she occupied.

It was overwhelming, the chemical smells. And far too bright for her liking.

There *had* been a peculiar odor, though. Something that reminded her of human sweat and fear.

A unique cacophony tickled her curiosity more. She glanced down the corridors, which were littered with slain humans. She had had her some fun. Only that there was no thrill to the hunt of such easy prey. If anything their panic and defenselessness made them a nuisance.

She killed them without taking more than a bite here and there, to appease her appetite. Even just a little. Her reason for killing them, though, was simple. Both ease and strategy.

The less humans running around, the less potential

threats.

And now this. A new sound.

Suddenly her nostrils flared.

An acquainted scent. She started to step forward, as her olfactory senses relayed the familiarity to her brain. Kilo. It was—

Kilo scrambled into view, from around a far corner. Projectiles zipped past her, faster than she could see, and one or two struck him as he tried to evade. They put a hitch in his step, as if the large male wasn't cumbersome enough in such close quarters.

Hestia hissed and leapt into the corridor, just as Kilo veered around a corner to dart down a perpendicular hall. The men wielding the projectile weapons shouted and adjusted their aim.

She warbled, piercing enough to reverberate down the hallway and the men clutched their ears.

She charged them, but one man moved past the others, and his weapon roared. Little projectiles sprayed her, but she was quick to dart after Kilo. A few struck her tail, not enough to draw blood. Just agitate the hide, and Hestia herself.

She grunted vehemently, and half-turned, wanting to retaliate. Her foot paused in a puddle of human blood, viscous and copious. She slid across the floor, righting herself and keeping from falling.

Kilo was quick to aid her, but she snapped at him, insistent she did not need the help. He snarled nonetheless, and turned to locate a stairwell. Descending it was a challenge without tumbling.

Hestia followed, noticing more than one flesh

wound adorning Kilo's green-and-brown body.

She was less than halfway down when a new sound stirred her attention. She paused, and turned.

In spite of everything that had transpired, how chaotically and terribly his plan had turned on itself, Dr. Lewis Campbell refused to harbor regret. He banished it from his cold heart, along with guilt and shame.

No, Campbell was pigheaded to hold onto nothing but pride and motivation.

Every experiment had to have its hiccups.

Surely his own security team would make corpses of the raptors—his prized subjects, a sad thing that would be—and then he could return.

To resume his work.

Isaacs was close at his heels. He would help.

Supposing they made it to the parking garage in one piece. Filled with a corrupt sense of optimism and immunity, the delusional Dr. Campbell led Glen Isaacs through hallways on the bottom level of the compound. The periodic sound of gunfire echoed across the building, both pleasing and worrying Campbell.

The fate of his personnel—Ida and Elijah's only assumed; others, whose corpses he and Isaacs walked by—was unfortunate.

But he was quick to remind himself of the omelet and eggs adage.

Elijah had insisted tagging along, but Campbell's assurance that the man would be safe inside the paddock lab got the best of him. Besides, neither the Doctor nor his loyal assistant were armed.

Sure, there were men with military experience wandering the compound who were, in fact, armed.

But Elijah wasn't too keen on waiting to cross paths with them, while any number of *Deinonychus* stalked the halls. Be it all six of them, or just a couple.

One on the loose, alone, sufficed to threaten Elijah's bladder to slacken.

He had at least locked—and even barricaded, with filing cabinets and desks—the only door into the lab. The glass windows overlooking the outdoor pen were high enough off the ground, and reinforced, to not worry him.

Sitting in a corner, curled up and muttering to himself, had started to dismantle his sanity. He heard gunfire at the other end of the building, this level by the sound of it. This reinvigorated him, and he leapt to his feet to begin assembling vital documents.

He knocked over a vial rack in the process, several test tubes shattering on the floor. The gunfire had ceased, and the silence shrouding the half-lit lab was unnerving by itself. He ended a gasp in his throat, and held his breath for several seconds before relaxing.

Or trying to.

Elijah realized he was on the verge of hyperventilating, and knew that he would serve no purpose by surviving this ordeal with a heart condition.

He paused, contemplating whether or not he should shred certain papers and delete certain files from the computer, or back them up to a secondary storage instead. Perhaps having some sort of leverage against the Doctor could help in the long run.

One of the small tables he had hoisted onto a filing

cabinet in front of the door suddenly shuddered before falling off. The filing cabinet rattled, metallic drawers making a heap of noise. The door itself buckled in the frame.

It was only then that Elijah Hall realized it was made of nothing but wood. Its heft, and steel frame, were its only comforts.

And suddenly the center of the door cracked, from an impact hard enough to topple one of the filing cabinets. Elijah choked on his breath as he staggered back, tripping over a trash bin.

The distinct, dull brown, reptilian snout of Hestia crashed through the door, followed by her enormous clawed hands, and she snarled a strident sound.

"Oh, God!" Elijah bawled, stumbling around a desk, papers flying in his wake.

Two seconds later the door buckled inward, and the immense frame of the female *Deinonychus* scrambled into the room.

Elijah screamed something incoherent as he found himself running toward the paddock windows. He couldn't compute why, but he quickly found himself gawking down at the very place that Hestia had previously been incarcerated.

And then her body slammed into him, her snout burying into his upper back. The reinforced glass splintered and shuddered in its frame, but held fast.

Hestia withdrew her skull, licking blood and pieces of cloth from her jaws. She peered over Elijah's right shoulder, as he groaned in pain, bleeding from a busted lip.

Her gaze descended.

The pen below. Its night-laden canopies and foliage. Everything planted artificially, to cater to a terrain befitting of her kind.

Her eyes acknowledged the inward-facing fences, and recalled their high-voltage properties.

Elijah groaned in pain between her and the glass. The weight of the raptor would soon crush his ribs, and his very regretful heart.

Hestia looked from the pen below to the human she had at her mercy. And then her scaly lips squirmed, as a purring growl exited her mouth. The man whimpered, and she lifted her right foot. The toe scythe dug into his right hip, puncturing muscle and bone.

His weak utterance pitched into a scream.

She caved in the back of his skull with her snout, savoring the kill almost more than the feast itself.

Scar's muzzle itched from the wound it had suffered. Something sharp had sliced it, at the hands of a human no less, and he was torn between annoyed and enraged. As if the little cuts he had endured during his attempt to breach that one small structure housing the two humans earlier wasn't enough.

Now he wandered the lower levels, having caught a whiff of Kilo at one point but quickly distracted by a fleeing human. He had pounced the woman and relished her screams almost as much as the blood beneath her blonde scalp.

Then a man shouted at him, and Scar heard the distinct sputter of electricity singe the air in front of him.

Somehow he had distracted himself so much with the kill that he had let a human—one he had come to know all too well—get absurdly close to him. The human blood lining his gums had even clotted his nostrils.

Aromatic as it was, Scar had unknowingly impaired his greatest sense.

He lifted his head, hissing at the man jabbing the electric baton at him. The human was snarling himself, in an inferior way, but Scar recognized the threat.

And then contact was made.

The baton knocked his snout, and a burst of voltage more than just shocked Scar. He chittered in pain and reeled back. He could have composed himself quicker than he did, though.

Scar wasn't as foolish as others would have him be. He toyed with that notion, and prepared to collapse, weak in the legs.

His handler chuckled, approached with a softer stance, before briskly lunging at him, baton sparking.

Juan Martín recognized the disfigured face of subject DA-08. "Scar," as some of the essential staff had come to call him. Martín insisted the creature wasn't worthy of a name. Best he see it as an animal to be tamed and trained, than an actual character.

Perhaps that was his greatest mistake.

Martín underestimated the beast.

Fell for its veneer of pain and weakness.

Suddenly Scar feigned, and Martín's baton missed its target. The raptor's jaws clamped around his arm, teeth puncturing bicep, triceps, and then grating down to hook his forearm. Blood was drawn in profuse rivulets. Martín screamed from an unprecedented pain. The baton clattered on the floor, harmless.

The same couldn't be said about the raptor.

Its bite force could have sundered Martín's arm from his shoulder, but instead the creature released him. He fell back, his arm hanging on by threads of flesh and intact bone, which he impulsively clutched at, only to wince in exacerbated pain.

A reddened, frothy hiss spewed from Scar's jaws, dappling the floor at Martín's feet.

Via his left earhole, he could hear the panting breaths of humans and their scurrying, ungainly feet. Like hooves on clumsy bipeds.

He lifted his head and turned it, in time to glimpse two humans scamper across the end of the corridor. Thirty feet away. And then they were gone. Heavy metal frames clanged in their wake. They had fled the building.

They believed they were safe.

Scar refocused on his present company. The man had ceased worrying about his mutilated arm—and started to reach for the baton. It would require more movement, maybe something drastic like a lunge.

Martín had acted slowly, not wanting to alert the raptor. Only then it was too late.

His eyes widened at the sight of the creature spotting him, its own split-pupil gaze narrowing on him.

And he knew his fate was sealed.

So Martín lunged for the baton on the floor, groaning from the pain in his arm. Whether or not he actually picked up the baton, he would never know. The raptor was upon him in a flash, both of its foot talons pinning him to the floor, their curved tips hooking his shoulder blades. His head jerked back, eyes clamped shut and every tactile sensation numbed.

Pain took over.

At least it was fleeting, from that point forward.

Martín received the same fatal blow that had befallen Channing Harbison, ironically enough by the same animal.

This didn't even register in Scar's mind.

At least not until he gulped down the warm, dense brain glop that reminded him of earlier.

Instead of savoring the rest of his kill, he wore a wicked smile, licking his coarse lips as he tucked his arms against his chest and darted down the corridor.

"Goddammit," Campbell muttered as he dropped his keys for the second time. It certainly didn't help that Isaacs was practically breathing down his neck, hands fidgeting nervously and repeatedly licking his lips to stay remotely hydrated.

Sure, Isaacs had his own car. But it was parked on the far end of the lot, and he deemed it more rational to carpool in a time like this.

"Why'd you park so damn far away?" Campbell asked, finally plunging the car key into the door lock.

He paused and glanced over his shoulder, regarding Isaacs with derision for once. The Doctor's self-appointed superiority was shining through the cracks.

Yet not even Isaacs, smart as the man was on most fronts, could not see it. Or at least didn't want to.

"S-Some *asshole* took my usual spot." Isaacs

scoffed, and indicated a large black pickup truck four spaces away. "I bet it was Gage, that prick. Or one of those Bravo—"

Campbell heard it even over Isaacs' rising voice. His assistant had somehow found a hint of equilibrium while venting a complaint. How trite.

The padded, rhythmic thumping of feet smacking pavement, carrying something large yet in such a light manner. This sound gradually reverberated through the parking garage, its clarity rapidly accelerating.

Campbell's eyes widened, realizing what it was. He had never heard the *Deinonychus* sprint across anything except soil, and seldom truly run, not beyond a short dash.

By the time his epiphany occurred, Isaacs catching on in that same belated moment, it was far too late for either of them. Especially Glen Isaacs.

The raptor used its stiff tail to help launch it airborne. It slammed into Isaacs from behind, and the yelping Dr. Campbell managed to reel back a split-second before his assistant's head crashed through the driver side window of his car. The alarm sounded, and Campbell rebounded off the tail end of another car, two spaces down.

His jaw hung open as he watched DA-08 gnash its teeth into Isaacs' lower back. His white lab coat was torn away in shreds of crimson, along with spare strips of flesh that escaped the raptor's jaws. One of its feet lifted to sink a claw into Isaacs' right thigh, and the femoral artery jetted blood across the pavement.

Isaacs screamed, and the fact that the man was still alive somehow motivated Campbell to do more than just stare in horror.

He turned and, babbling, ran.

The raptor he recognized as Scar withdrew from Isaacs, whose body remained half-inside his boss's car, shards of glass stuck in his face and scalp.

Even over his own heaving breaths, Campbell could hear the raptor's. They were louder, gruffer, and filled with an incomparable malice. Their echo in the parking garage elaborated the fear that hearing them incited.

Asthma which Campbell had not known in over a decade suddenly returned to his lungs and tightened around his throat.

A car reversed suddenly before him, its tires shrieking against the pavement. He struck the side of it and bounced off, losing his balance at the same time. Whoever the driver was, he could not tell, was dead-set on making it out of there.

The sedan spun around, pausing briefly so the driver could slam it into drive, while Campbell struggled to shout at them. From the ground. He had sprained his ankle and found himself incapable of standing without feeling a searing pain in his leg.

His palms were scraped and his glasses had fallen from his face.

Lewis Campbell had never felt more dehumanized, much less unworthy of his Doctor credit.

Yet he remained devoid of regret.

Haughty of his achievements.

And, if even infinitesimally, hopeful he would make it out of this alive. To salvage his career. And, in turn, his life.

This arrogance would not survive his death.

But first Scar leapt onto the hood of the car, claws scraping metal and denting it beneath him. The driver inside screamed and reflexively struck their horn. The sound briefly disoriented him, and he darted over the vehicle. His claws left puncture marks in the windshield, roof, and rear window. Then it alighted onto the pavement behind the car, which proceeded to peel off.

"No, no, no," Campbell whimpered, reaching out for the car.

A tear hit the concrete upon which he awkwardly sat. And then a glob of saliva. It was pinkish. Sullied by blood.

And not the raptor's.

Campbell peered up at Scar, its face appearing worse than ever. Suggesting it had been wounded by a variety of elements since the Doctor last saw it.

He really *had* achieved something here.

Creating genuinely terrifying, absolutely imposing beasts. Resurrecting from extinction wasn't enough. Campbell needed to one-up God and make his own alterations.

Now those very same variances glared down at him, licking its lips.

Campbell raised a hand a moment before the raptor gnashed down at his face. As if that would suffice. But Scar's teeth simply tore away most of his hand, from the base of his fingers to the knob of his wrist. Severed digits sprinkled the pavement, followed by beads of blood. And then a heavier splash, from his spurting wrist.

A scream tapered off at his lips as Campbell gawked at his own terrible wound.

Scar's toe claws tapped the pavement as he savored the taste, and the helplessness of the human below him. He had heard this particular one speak to him before, a dialect he didn't understand, but the inflection was easy enough to dissect.

This human was in charge.

Or had been.

Scar shrieked at him, a trilling sound that scrambled Campbell's brain and made him reflexively cover his ears. Only that one of his hands never made it. Instead he smeared his own blood across his cheek, and began to sob in defeat.

Perhaps it was then that his arrogance disintegrated.

Or maybe it wasn't until Scar was eating him alive, piece by piece, his own creation somehow not disappointing.

<u>9</u>

With the tables turned, the five men felt the best they had all night. It wasn't just their ample armaments, although that definitely helped. From shotguns to pistols and pockets full of shells all around. Gage had even resupplied Armijo the keys to his truck, and distributed ear protection. But beyond all of this was the irony. That they were now hunting the very beasts which had previously been hunting them. Only they knew not to let it get to their heads. Despite their military experience, there was no veteran in any field that could compare to this situation.

Gage had put it best once the big one evaded them, and joined with an even larger raptor in the upper hallways.

"I've seen these things function in captivity. They were raised and mistreated to enhance aggression. But that's not all. They aren't passive animals by nature. So don't underestimate their prowess. I might not know all the details of their IQ tests, but one thing's clear."

He then turned to more directly address the four survivors of Bravo.

"These creatures have millions of years' worth of honed instincts in their genes. We got nothing on that. So stay sharp."

Although Gage didn't pride himself in lecturing the

men, already filled with the guilt of taking their weapons under Campbell's orders and in a manner of speaking being responsible for their casualties, he felt they were past that.

At least from a tactical, heat-of-the-moment standpoint. Later, supposing they survived this ordeal, he imagined the men might not ever want to speak with him again.

And he would understand.

Besides, Gage would have to endure his own arduous self-reconciliation for the loss of Anderssen. A man he had known since before boot, back when he called him nothing but Tate, had not met a painless demise. This much was evident when they finally came across his body in a bathroom on the second floor.

One of the raptor handlers, Alec Carter, had been split down the back and was missing half of his face, lying in a pool of his own blood, outside the bathroom.

The men of Bravo recognized the grief on Gage, especially Labella and Guidry, who wore a similar shade.

A distant clamor pulled them out of this mournful stupor. It was a sound both puzzling and familiar at the same time. It took the men only a few seconds before realizing it was a car alarm.

"Parking garage," Armijo and Fletcher said, simultaneously.

"I bet the Good Doctor is trying to make it out clean," Labella said, bitterly.

"Fat chance," Gage said, and gestured with his head for the men to follow him toward the nearest stairwell. They turned a corner and Gage indicated that it was at the far end, about eighty feet down.

A new sound tickled their ears before they got farther than a few feet, and the group paused to listen. For all they knew, it could be someone calling for help. Or talking to themselves, praying, behind a door somewhere.

Surely there were survivors…

Gage recognized it before the others. His eyes widened. It was the purring of a nearby *Deinonychus*. He didn't need to voice this for the others to register it. Their heads swiveled, heels pivoting. Guns sweeping—

A strident yet guttural, trilling roar that was like a cross between a viper's hiss, a jaguar's growl, and a vulture's squawk, cut through the air. It was close, but how near they couldn't tell. Near enough to disorient them from volume alone.

It was punctuated by the panicked shouting of a man who proceeded to careen around a corner at the opposite end of the hall they occupied. It seemed that the man had risen up the stairwell from the ground level, and was now bolting in their direction.

Although Bravo had met Dr. Campbell, Glen Isaacs, and their on-site security team, that was it.

So none of them recognized who Gage immediately realized was Seamus O'Connor. His dark red hair was disheveled, and blood painted half of his face. The raptor handler's right sleeve was gone, exposing a nasty gash that ran the length of his bicep, and cascaded blood down his forearm.

This didn't hinder his mobility, fortunately.

Until of course O'Connor tripped on a med-tech's corpse, and stumbled. He would have righted himself had his boot not stomped half a spilt liver, and his legs went out beneath him.

The men watched him fall, tumbling across the floor about forty feet away. And another forty, behind him, manifested one of the larger raptors. It was dark green and brown—

Without a hitch in its step.

The massive creature's body streamlined as it charged down the hall.

Every one of them had a pistol in their possession. They each swapped the shotgun from their hands to open fire with the pistols, a mix of 9mm and .45-caliber rounds volleying the raptor head-on. It slalomed on approach of the scampering O'Connor, whimpering as he feared the worst.

It didn't help that he was getting to his feet.

Someone accidentally clipped him in the shoulder, as he rose up during the gunfire. His body spun and the group immediately ceased shooting, scattered profanity under their breaths.

Labella abandoned their group not to flee, but charge forward. He even dropped his pistol out of frustration, likely assuming it was he who accidentally shot the man.

Carrying the Remington across his chest, he ran and was mindful of his footing, unlike O'Connor.

The raptor had managed to evade more than half of their gunfire, but it still bled from an array of wounds. Somehow this barely hindered the beast, and it was upon O'Connor before Labella could achieve a clean shot.

Even as he yelled at him to drop.

"Get down, down!" Labella shouted, waving.

His boots caught a blood puddle and slid across the tile, but didn't lose his footing. Labella snapped the shotgun's butt up to his shoulder, holding it tight, and fingered the trigger.

The featherless, reptilian *Deinonychus* still had its avian form down to a T. Such a sight was nothing shy of awe-inspiring, in every fashion.

Its jaws gnashed at O'Connor's throat, from behind, its toe claws dug into his calves and its taloned hands gripping his waist, keeping him afoot.

Labella watched blood shoot from his mouth, eyes wide.

The poor man mouthed a single word.

Even through the frothing blood, Labella could discern it. From the s to the h, the two o's and the—

T.

Labella's shotgun opened up. The cluster of 12-gauge buckshot caught the raptor in the head, held so snugly between O'Connor's neck and right shoulder. It shrieked and recoiled, shaking its head in pain. O'Connor's body dropped, his right ear shredded by spare pellets. His nose broke upon colliding with the floor, and he proceeded to asphyxiate on his own blood.

Labella racked the shotgun on fast approach, while his comrades hustled to his right, to attend O'Connor.

The raptor turned away to flee, and Labella slammed a tight grouping of buckshot into its right hip. The already injured beast staggered, blood spraying the floor. It released a painful yelp and wobbled forward nonetheless, crashing through a door.

Angrily racking the shotgun again, Labella ejected a spent shell that clattered across the floor, trailing a wisp of smoke. Labella's nose wrinkled, his face distorted not from the acridity of gunfire but from…

Everything else.

"He's gone, he's…hey!" Armijo had to practically shove Guidry off of O'Connor's corpse.

Guidry didn't even know the man, but felt for him immensely. And was all the more aggravated that they, despite their firepower and numbers, could not save him. That previously conquered feeling of futility returned to Guidry like a rabid linebacker. It knocked the breath from his lungs and left him dazed.

Armijo nudged Fletcher before rising to his feet, to catch up to Labella. The man was pursuing the raptor toward the room into which it had fled.

Meanwhile, Fletcher attempted to console Guidry, and reel him back to reality. The present. However unenticing it was.

The exchange seemed familiar.

Both men remembered the horrors in their trailers earlier. This helped Guidry refocus quicker.

He would loathe himself if his inability to handle the situation got someone else killed.

It was then that Guidry looked to his right and watched Armijo attempt to hold Labella back, from entering a room.

And following the raptor.

He pushed past Fletcher and ran for the men, hopeful to catch Labella before he did something stupid. His booted footfalls echoing in the hall. Perhaps that was what the raptor homed in on, from a room within the room that Labella was about to enter. The drywall to Guidry's right erupted in a mist of white dust, and the giant raptor, in spite of its wounds, collided with him.

Guidry hit the opposite wall and rebounded directly into the raptor's clutches. A claw swiped his gut, but a ballistic vest kept him from being disemboweled. If only he had been wearing a helmet—

And even then, nothing was certain.

The others were reeling from the abrupt, unexpected breach of the raptor through the wall when its jaws gnashed at Guidry's face. He had not retrieved his shotgun since attending O'Connor, so he was genuinely defenseless.

Except for a pistol.

Even as Guidry's face was torn away from him, first a cheekbone and then an eye from its lacerated socket, he drew the pistol just enough to rapidly squeeze the trigger. One after another, .45-caliber bullets punched through the raptor's left leg and foot.

It wobbled, pausing from devouring its prey.

So much for entirely helpless.

By this time the others had reoriented and Labella reemerged from the room to blast at the raptor's right leg with his shotgun. The creature fell, and Guidry staggered back, missing half of his face. A cut in his jugular was one more wound that his free hand could not tend to. Although, he didn't really try. Guidry's right hand continued to fire the pistol at the fallen, bleeding raptor.

Even as the life squirmed from his own veins.

Kilo twitched and whimpered in defeat, there on the floor, surrounded by humans.

Still waiting for Hestia to launch her coup.

Not realizing, or would ever come to know, that she had been distracted by another human. While flanking the backside of the group they had detected earlier, from below, a survivor attempting to flee the building caught her nose.

She hissed and attacked the woman, who was unable to scream before Hestia's jaws tilted and locked around her neck. Slightly curved, terrifically sharp teeth not only punctured her throat on both sides, but also sawed through, before crushing the woman's larynx. Her head bobbed backward, neck connected solely by a scarred spinal column.

Hestia crouched over her victim, lapping up the flesh and briefly distracted by her own appetite. And her own little victory.

For Hestia was, ultimately, an animal at her core. Nature had its way, and for a flawed moment she had forgotten about Kilo.

His death, however, she would not take lightly. Whether it was an emotional response or a consequence that directly affected her species' survival, the reason was irrelevant.

"Christ Almighty, what the fuck is…" Gage paused to knead his forehead, and then slap himself in the side of the head. He was panged with grief and anger, the latter being directed inwardly more than at the raptor itself, for Guidry's death.

He was still kneeling by the man, while his actual friends and brothers-in-arms struggled to compartmentalize the loss in the moment.

"Hey, we need to go," Armijo insisted, tugging at Gage's arm.

He shook it off and continued to mutter to himself, shaking his head. He had since removed his hat, flinging it across the hall in frustration. His ponytail remained intact, while sweat gleamed his forehead.

Everyone was all but doused in it.

Not to mention Guidry's and O'Connor's blood on their hands.

Metaphorically, too, as far as Gage was concerned. Pulling himself out of that stupor would be easier said than done.

Which was why it took a second raptor's appearance to do the job. The creature veering around the corner behind them barely made a sound, until it was already halfway to them. Then its heavy footfalls and shrill panting became unavoidable.

Somehow they heard the beast before any of them actually saw it, which wasn't exactly inconspicuous.

Its length and mass was even more than the one they had just killed. It was also a darker coloration, a dull brown, unlike all the other creatures.

Everything pointed to *bad.*

"Go, go, go, the stairs!" Armijo shouted, as the others ran, more on impulse than his command.

He literally lifted Gage from where he knelt, and turned to fire at the creature. Armijo was a tall, sturdy man; brawny in his prime, and although that was behind him now, he was still in great shape.

Gage was a solid figure, too, but a few inches shorter and not as built.

Still, he managed to knock Armijo back, taking his place and firing at the impending creature. Armijo stumbled over the dead raptor and braced himself against the gaping hole through which it had come.

Gage got off two fast rounds from his pistol before the beast struck him, albeit slowing to strike his chest with the top of its head. It had taken both rounds to the torso, which it didn't care for.

The brunt-force impact threw Gage down the hall, and he landed awkwardly, before tumbling head-over-heels. He dislocated his shoulder in the process, grimacing. His pistol skittered across the floor.

Armijo fired at the raptor, far too close for comfort, and the muzzle flash alone disoriented the creature, in tandem with the ringing sound. The bullet itself must have passed between its jaws, hitting nothing but the opposite wall.

It swung its body around, tail nearly taking off Armijo's head had he not ducked. And rolled, away. In the fray he had survived with neither pistol nor shotgun, despite stuffed pockets of ammunition. Instead of lunging for them, adrenaline powered him onward, hoisting Gage to his feet and helping him to the stairwell.

There, Fletcher aimed his pistol down the hall, waiting for a clear shot. Unfortunately by the time he had one, it lasted half a second, and then the big raptor was gone, making a turn and heading elsewhere.

Likely to try flanking them some other way.

The men knew the creature would not give up so easily, especially with a fellow raptor slain, and having been injured itself.

They stumbled down the steps, Gage wincing all the while, but helped to move by Armijo. Meanwhile Labella led with his shotgun, and Fletcher at his heels, wielding the only pistol left among them.

How it had come to this was deeply unsettling. Their morale was mutilated, but their lives were not yet forfeit.

Even if Guidry's, among others', were.

They made it to the front of the compound, its foyer a large, open lobby. The reception desk was a circular structure that, in their minds, didn't seem to serve much of a purpose given the secrecy of this installation.

Nonetheless, they used it to catch their breath.

"We can't…wait here," Gage panted.

"Cool your jets," Fletcher said, joining Armijo to help relocate Gage's shoulder. The man gnashed his teeth and handled the pain better than expected.

"Consider them cooled." Gage caught his breath. "Can we…can we go now?"

"Righty-o," Fletcher said, and let Armijo handle him. Gage insisted he could walk on his own, but knew he would not be able to properly use that arm for a while.

In the meantime, Labella cautiously approached the metallic double-doors. Their push-bar handles. wouldn't depress. He tried again, attempting to be quiet, but they wouldn't budge.

He turned to face the others on approach.

"Building's on lockdown," Gage said. "Need a

code. Over there. Enter 1-9-8-4."

"How poetic," Fletcher muttered.

Labella shook his head and brushed tears from his face, recalling Guidry and the others, without even wanting to. He located the keypad beside the doors and inputted the code.

"Let's get the fuck outta here."

The parking garage was a straight shot, more or less. The sidewalk that was paved across the grass, at an obtuse angle from the access road leading to the garage itself, extended before them. They took the ramp instead of the steps, as it was a more direct route.

Nightfall was still in its earliest hours, and it would be darkest for a while longer.

Fortunately the parking garage remained illuminated, this glow of light providing a nimbus that casted over half the sidewalk.

They crossed vigilantly, but not gingerly.

Fear bred haste.

10

Unlike his past victims of the night, Scar didn't relent from his most recent until he had his fill. Then he left the corpse and returned to the other vehicle, hauling the body out with his jaws. The alarm had since stopped, thankfully, but shortly after beginning his proper feast, it kicked up again. Startling him. He recoiled, snorting, and ultimately ripped one of the dead man's legs off at the knee, taking it with him.

As far from the damn clamor as he could.

He was twelve vehicles down, at the end of this aisle, when he dropped the leg and began gnawing through the flesh. His teeth scraped bone, tickling his gums and delighting his brain.

Scar paused to lift his head and survey the larger building. It occurred to him that the others might need his help.

The notion that the big and mighty Hestia, or Kilo, would actually need *his* assistance immediately amused him. He shook his head and returned his snout to the thickest part of the leg. The meaty thigh.

Delicious.

He was about through it when he heard the car alarm cut off again. What a relief. Yet only then did he hear something else, in the thick silence. Voices overlapping, their dialect obscure to him—but not alien. He recognized the inflections as human, and immediately after this came the scent.

At first it was subtle.

And then it built.

His nostrils flared. He perked up, his form rising from behind a car, and he tilted his head. Another snort preceded a growl.

A group of humans.

A herd. Attempting to escape, like the ones before them. Like the ones that Scar had killed, joyously.

Because Scar was the keeper.

And he would not let these flee, either.

He would feast more.

Until he couldn't move, until his belly ached and his gums thickened with human flesh.

"Kill that fucking alarm," Gage rasped. Fletcher was already on it, handing Armijo his pistol. He opened the car door, trying to ignore the dismembered body of Glen Isaacs, not to mention all the crumbs of shattered glass and blood inside the vehicle.

He pulled a cluster of wiring down from under the steering column and yanked the necessary ones out.

The alarm whimpered off.

Fletcher emerged, and then whistled under his breath. The others saw, too. Campbell's corpse a few spaces to their left.

"What a shame," Armijo said. "I was really hoping to be the one."

"Better than no karma at all," Labella said. He nod-ded toward the compound. "Just look at what happened here."

"Well, not everyone was nuts in there."

"How do you figure?" Fletcher asked Armijo. "I mean, besides Gage here. And his men."

Gage nodded, showing some mute appreciation for the gesture.

"Remember that call I got," Armijo said. There was some puzzlement amid the group, but he didn't go into it. "Regardless, this whole thing is a travesty."

"Can't argue with that," Fletcher said.

"There's our truck," Labella's voice gained some enthusiasm. He gestured at the large black pickup four spaces down. The ones between it and the car whose alarm Fletcher disabled were empty. Down this row of vehicles were six more, across twice as many spaces.

Labella rushed to the truck, and was tossed the keys by Armijo. They knew that without Gage, they would have died back outside warehouse, which felt like hours upon hours ago, but was probably no more than one or two.

And without him, they would have never had the gear with which they used to protect themselves. Albeit a little fruitlessly, it had saved their asses on more than one instance.

Even killed one of the biggest of the creatures.

Now, Labella subconsciously acknowledged Gage's contribution to the moment he turned the key in the ignition. Not that Fletcher couldn't hot-wire the truck, or any vehicle for that matter, but this was—

A warbling cry down the parking garage.

—*Easier*.

"Get in, get in!" Armijo shouted, rushing Gage to be pulled into the truck's backseat by Fletcher. They succeeded, while another raptor—smaller than the other two but not enough to diminish their fear—bounded toward them. Instead of darting down the aisle of cars, it used the vehicles' rooftops, leaping from one to the other.

Some of the smaller vehicles' roofs were crushed by its passing weight, windows shattering in its wake. The creature drastically approached, evading all but one of Armijo's last-effort shots, before the pistol's slide locked back.

The one that hit had merely grazed the creature, by which time it trilled shrilly before making a desperate pounce from three spaces away. It landed in the bed of the large truck, its V8 idling, chassis now bouncing and whining under the beast's weight.

Upon a closer look, it had clearly already suffered various wounds before this encounter. It bled all over, and had a distinctly aged scar down the side of its cut-up face.

Armijo wasn't the only one to recognize the raptor. In the backseat, gawking at it through the rear window, Gage and Fletcher were speechless.

Labella glimpsed it in the rearview, as it roared and savored all of their fear. He recalled the very same snout, which had killed Hsu and Harbison.

Even with Armijo outside the truck, Labella impulsively punched the gas. In reverse. The pickup lurched back, just as Armijo finished reloading. Labella's door was still open, and Armijo had to leap back to avoid getting hit by it.

The raptor briefly lost its footing, tumbling forward, its head crashing through the back window. Inside, Fletcher and Gage cried out, wishing they were armed.

Except Fletcher was.

He unsheathed his knife and plunged three of the four inches into the creature's slender neck. It bucked and wailed, pulling free of the window.

Labella hit the brakes and the raptor was flung out of the truck. It tumbled across the pavement, just as its larger, brown-scaled cohort arrived.

"Fuck me," Armijo muttered, and then swallowed every emotional burden. He raised the pistol in both hands and unleashed in the two creatures' direction.

The big one evaded, swifter on its feet than something that size ought to be. Bullets struck the concrete pillar it darted by, trilling loudly as it went.

Before he knew it, the pistol's slide locked back and his pocket was empty.

Labella shouted at Armijo from the driver's seat. His words scraped out of his parched throat, but Armijo heard him clearly enough.

"Shotgun! On your left!"

Armijo dropped the pistol and lunged for the shotgun Labella had left behind.

"Behind you!" The men in the backseat shouted, their voices overlapping.

Armijo turned as the scar-faced raptor leapt at him. The shotgun blasted it midair, pellets shearing through the meat of its already injured neck. Fletcher's knife was still in it before the wound gaped, and blood carried the raptor's life force out of it.

A clawed foot twitched briefly where it had collapsed on the pavement.

Armijo racked the slide but the chamber was empty. He cursed under his breath and fished out new shells from a pocket.

"Get in, goddammit!" Labella yelled.

The sound of the raptor's approach was tumultuous. It approached from the truck's right, in the same fashion that its smaller predecessor had. Car to car. Even more windows shattered this time around, as the beast itself was about the size of a Porsche.

Armijo had loaded two shells when he abandoned the effort and launched himself toward the truck. Labella shut his door and spun the wheel, seconds before Armijo vaulted up the back left wheel and fell into the bed. Spare tools and a polyester tarp "cushioned" his landing.

Suddenly the massive *Deinonychus*, its brown hide shimmering under the fluorescent ceiling fixtures in the parking garage, launched itself airborne.

Labella whipped the truck around, facing its direction. It barely made the turn before the creature landed, notably clawed feet buckling the windshield and spraying glass dust into the cabin. Labella choked and squinted, partially blind as he veered the truck and accelerated.

The vehicle's chassis groaned, raptor hand-claws scoring the roof above Fletcher and Gage's heads. A toe sickle punctured the windshield for purchase, and another stabbed the hood of the truck. The creature roared, its split-pupil amber eyes glaring down at Armijo in the bed.

"Eat this," he growled, and fired the shotgun, nearly point-blank.

The raptor's face was all but shorn away, and its body tumbled off the truck. The vehicle teetered on its left tires, before the weight of the creature's collapse pulled it the rest of the way. It landed on one of its legs, crushing both its tibia and fibula. It wailed out in pain, but that wasn't all.

Hestia could not fathom her defeat. The humans had been more abundant, but far less capable. Their technology and teamwork had miraculously conquered her intelligence, the efforts of her cohorts, and even the rapacious vengeance of Scar.

She blamed her own bestial faults for Kilo's death, and in turn hers.

However, not all hope was vanquished from Hestia's subconscious. What awaited her on the other side of this existence was beyond her understanding. She wondered if it would compare to the freedom that was sprawled out before Victor and Six.

Amid her dying breaths, she envisioned them on the other side of the perimeter fence, enjoying the liberties of an uncaged life.

11

Ida's departure from the compound, and in many ways a version of prison for her, was slow and apprehensive. Every step a pain to take, not physically but emotionally. The sights of utter bloodshed she beheld agonized her soul, and she couldn't help but feel a fraction of responsibility.

The closer she got to the front lobby, the nearer her escape, the fiercer the guilt.

Alas she clung to one of the doors and sobbed.

If she were caught by a roaming raptor and brutally slain in this moment of human weakness, Ida wouldn't necessarily fault herself for it. Part of her mind saw the justice in it.

And then a sound snagged her attention, one that wasn't bestial. The whirring of tires against pavement, unable to achieve traction. An engine redlining, without shifting gears.

Her brow furrowed and she shifted her body to push the door open. It had not been shut all the way. Her initial stumble into the open and down the path toward the parking garage was frightful and reluctant.

As her tears cleared and her view of the structure aligned, her pace quickened. She almost tripped on herself, wanting to discard her pumps but fearful of walking across glass or other debris.

Ida's eyes widened upon approach.

Scar's corpse, and ten feet from it, an overturned pickup truck. The tires spun relentlessly, the engine climbing with nowhere to go. This cycle intermittently stopped and continued. Stopped and continued.

She rushed around to the top side.

She didn't know their names, but the men were clearly security. Cillian Gage, she recognized. He was in the process of trying to pull the driver away from the concrete upon which he rested, his door flattened against it. Shards from his shattered window were stuck in his left arm like nasty splinters, but it seemed he had protected his face enough.

The dark-skinned driver's feet sporadically pumped the gas pedal. Until finally Gage, with the help of another man, heavily bearded and wearing a tactical vest, hoisted the driver into the upturned bed, through the shattered rear window. The rectangular space was narrow but feasible.

Ida finally broke from her daze and attempted to help. Movement behind her made her flinch. A tall, robust man with cuts on his face and arms, a goatee and blood clearly someone else's on his hands, had stood up from the truck bed. She had not even noticed him before.

He nodded at her, mute, but moved to help the others.

She looked around in the meantime, or started to, until his voice startled her. She turned back to face him, and began to shake her head.

"Is it dead?" He repeated, his voice deep and husky. Something about it familiar.

"W-What?"

"The thing. The raptor. Is it dead?" He asked, sounding completely out of it. Exhaustion compounded by pain, grief, fear, and, just possibly, hope.

All of this was legible on his face alone.

"Scar is, he's..." She thumbed over her shoulder, brow furrowing. She started to say something, and then noticed the heap of brown scales and blood on the other side of the truck cab. She flinched and brought a hand to her mouth. "Oh my God. Hestia. She's..."

"*She*?" The bearded man asked, looking up from Gage and the driver. The latter of whom was regaining full awareness, wincing from his injuries. The bearded man scoffed. "That figures."

"It. She. Whatever." The tall man before her shook his head and peered past her to briefly observe Hestia's body. Then he withdrew. "Looks dead to me. Oughtta be. Took a 12-gauge, point-blank to the face."

"If that didn't do it, then I quit," Gage mumbled, running a tattered hand and fingers through his hair. The ponytail came loose and he took ragged breaths.

"We're good," the tall man said, squatting beside the others and vigorously patting Gage's shoulder. He winced. The man half-smirked. "Sorry, brother."

Gage looked up at him.

"Wait, you're..." Ida half-gasped and half-rejoiced. "You're the one I spoke to on the phone! Bravo. You're—"

"Armijo. Eric." He stood and faced Ida, offering his hand. "I appreciate your head's up. Wish I'd been more...receptive."

"You can't blame yourself for a magnitude of disbelief," she replied, tears welling beneath her eyes. "I'm Ida. Ida Sala—"

"Can we go home now?" One of them muttered. She didn't see which, but imagined it was on all of their minds.

That and pay.

Not that any amount of money could mend what was lost here, but it was a start. For them, and for their casualties' families.

"Do you…do you know where Lewis Campbell is?" Ida asked.

Armijo smirked, dryly. "I like that you didn't say *Doctor*."

"He doesn't deserve that title after what he's done. None of us ever will."

"Well, for starters," the bearded man said, rising to his feet. He didn't offer his hand, but he did bow his head briefly, and mutter "Fletcher, ma'am," before continuing. "Campbell's dead. And so is Isaacs. If you look to your left, on down a little ways, you'll…"

She did, and gasped, covering her mouth.

"Oh my God," she muttered. It wasn't quite grief. Something else. Disgust, and a fleck of relief. That she had not suffered the same fate.

"Look, Ida, is it?" Fletcher said, sounding oddly upbeat. She understood; the adrenaline was still pumping, and that some men in their profession handled stress with excess cheer wasn't unusual. "I know this is gonna be one helluva cesspool of investigations and lawsuits, but for now we'd all really love a cold shower and about a week's worth of sleep."

"At least," the driver groaned.

"Not to mention burying our friends," Armijo stepped forward, his voice firmer than before. "And struggling to grasp how in the *fuck* we're going to console their families."

Ida gulped. "I…I understand, I…I mean, we should get going. I have my keys. My car's small, but we'll manage."

She looked around frantically.

Silence palled the parking garage. In its transient stillness, a sound could be heard in the distance. Almost like lightning, but without the thunder. And fainter. Then another sound, awfully familiar.

Awfully, indeed.

"Oh, no," Ida muttered, her heart sinking into her gut. "Oh, God, no."

"What, what is it?" Armijo asked, brow furrowed. He looked around.

Gage read the dismay on her face and then struggled to his feet.

He proceeded to look around.

A dizzying fear made him wobble. Fletcher was quick to support him.

"Can someone please—"

"The other two," Gage said. He coughed into his hand, and then stared, wide-eyed, at Armijo. "The smaller ones. Y-You said earlier, that they, they split up. Went to the fence."

"The *fence*?" Ida gasped. "No, no. W-Which two?"

"Victor and Six, I think," Gage said.

Ida felt faint. She braced herself against the overturned truck bed.

"The fence is electrified, but the gate isn't," she finally said.

Everyone stared at each other.

"It's not just that," she said, lip quivering.

"What could be worse?" Armijo's brow furrowed. He looked around for the shotgun, and went to retrieve it.

Gage shook his head. Armijo hated to see it, not just the gesture but the look in his eyes. That it was already too late.

And then Ida spoke. And as she did, that hope they had recently unearthed began to shrink away again.

"Hestia, the big one there, was female. She was the *only* female. All the others were engineered with protandrous hermaphrodism." She read the men's blank faces. "They could…*can*…switch to female, in a single-sex environment, to reproduce. To save their species."

"What?" Fletcher practically laughed. "Why in the hell would—"

"Campbell was drunk on power. Never stopping to question whether he should, intoxicated by the fact that he *could*. And Isaacs was his lap-dog. We were all…distracted by his genius. His…" Ida felt nauseous. "Insanity."

"So what are you saying?" Armijo pressed. "That if those two get out into the world, they'll start multiplying?"

"Not if," she said, her voice weak. "But when."

Victor and Six nipped at each other after alighting on the

hard ground. Bypassing the gate had proven easier than finding a weakness in the perimeter fence, and they regretted not trying it sooner.

Beneath their coarse hide, soft tissue still itched with residual electricity.

The cacophony from the main building, and the smaller, illuminated structure nearby, suggested that they might be alone now.

Returning to check on the others seemed like too much of a risk. Especially since neither Hestia nor Kilo had come back to call on them.

If they weren't needed, it was likely because the others had already conquered the property. Or been conquered themselves.

Victor and Six's toe claws tapped the asphalt and their gazes swept the treeline forty feet in front of them. The forest seemed to extend for quite a ways. Miles, possibly more, in both directions.

Six glanced back.

Victor nudged the raptor and purred, prancing across the road and vanishing into the woods. When Six looked forward again, he was alone. But he could smell Victor, among a smorgasbord of other scents.

Stomach growling, Six ran off to follow Victor into the wooded, fenceless pen of freedom.

* 9 7 9 8 9 9 9 4 5 5 0 8 8 5 *